Like a Brother

Maurice M. Gray, Jr.

WRITE THE VISION

Published by Write The Vision
Box 13083 Wilmington, DE 19850
(302) 765-8709
E-mail: writevision2000@yahoo.com
Web site: www.writethevision.biz

Gray, Maurice M, Jr.
    Like A Brother by Maurice M. Gray, Jr.

ISBN-13: 978-0-9700514-1-7
ISBN- 0-9700514-1-7

First printing: April 2016

Printed in the U.S.A.

ACKNOWLEDGEMENTS

Here I am again! My first solo work in years, but it feels like I never stopped.

This is the part that can get a brother in trouble-acknowledgements! I try to mention everybody, but someone gets left out and I have to pray for no hurt feelings. If that someone was you this time around, chalk it up to me being in my mid-forties and therefore prone to forget stuff.

I thank God for giving me creativity and the ability to use it. I can't think of a better way to spend my time.

To my family, particularly my father Maurice M. Gray, Sr. and my sister Rev. Regina Gray, thank you! It means a lot when I mention that I'm working on a new book and your first response is to tell me to hurry up and finish it so you can have something new to read. Uncle Joe, Aunt Jackie and my fifty-eleven cousins on that side of the family, thank you for relentlessly asking for and promoting my books

Dr. Linda Beed, thank you as always for your critical eye when I needed feedback and for your constant encouragement when I didn't want to read this not ONE more time ☺.

Thank you Pastor (soon to be Bishop!) Silvester Scott Beaman and my Bethel African Methodist Episcopal Church family for supporting me unconditionally.

Fellow authors, you keep me going. There are too many of you to name; this is only a fraction of those who inspire and encourage me. ReShonda Tate Billingsley, Parker Cole, Sharon Ewell Foster, Pat G'orge-Walker, Patricia Haley-Glass, Jeanette Hill, LaShaunda Hoffman, Kendra Holmes, Derek Jackson, Kevin Wayne Johnson, Terrance Johnson, E.N. Joy, Tyora Moody, Victoria Christopher Murray, Leslie Sherrod, Michelle Stimpson, Jacquelin Thomas and the list goes on and on.

Thank you to my writers group, the First State Scribes! Regina

Bumbrey, Nichole Christopoulos, Desiree Cox, Christine Pauls, Joreen Schatze Sykes and S. Raven Storm, you rock!

My brothers of Kappa Alpha Psi Fraternity, Inc., who always encourage me to achieve even greater things with each new accomplishment

Elissa Gabrielle and my fellow contributors to The Soul Of A Man and The Soul Of A Man 2: Make Me Wanna Holler anthologies. Soul Brothers, I'm enjoying getting to know you all. Let's continue to be about our Father's business as we promote them properly.

Dedication

I dedicate this book to my parents. Without their love, support and guidance, I wouldn't have been able to accomplish such a massive undertaking. I love you both.

Maurice M. Gray, Sr.

You gave me life and your name. Thank you for teaching me the meaning of the words "work ethic," and for showing me how a Christian man is supposed to conduct himself.

Joan K. Gray (6/18/36-8/8/05)

Thank you for instilling within me a deep appreciation for the written word. You taught me from an early age to love reading, which led me to love writing as well. I'll miss you until we meet again.

1

"I caught the bouquet!"

Like she should be surprised. Jenisse wasn't gonna be denied; she boxed out like a WNBA power forward on a mission. Forget Elena Delle Donne and Brittney Griner- she would have taken down LeBron James with that move.

I decided to give her a bit of wit instead of my real thoughts. "Good! That means you're next to get married and you're out of my hair."

Jenisse threw a weak punch at my shoulder.

"Uh uh Jay, you don't get rid of me that easy. At least not unless that guy catches the garter."

I turned in the direction of her head lean. I didn't know this guy, but I hated him already. I hated him because basketball player tall, Hollywood actor looking brothers weren't high on my list. I hated him more because Jenisse drooled over those types to the point of worship.

I gave him another once-over and wondered what he had that I didn't. The answer was simple—he had her full attention.

"They're about to throw it, Jay. You should get over there and make sure my future husband is the only one with a chance to snag it!"

Like I'm gonna help the competition.

Jenisse pulled me to where the unwilling horde of single men straggled into place and wedged me in between her man in her head and the groom's cousin. She slipped off to the chair reserved for the bouquet catcher to wait. When the garter was tossed, Fantasy Man accidentally deflected it right to me.

"Your girl caught the bouquet, dawg. You need that more than I do."

I reaped the reward for Fantasy Man's largesse. Jenisse's pout vanished when I gave in to the urge to get her back for hyping him at my expense. I did a "Best Man" move on her and slid the garter up as high as I possibly could without showing her goodies to the assembled crowd. When I tickled her knee, she almost kicked me in the face.

Tickling her was a big mistake, and not just because of her doctor's office reflex. That kick allowed a split-second panty-peek that brought back memories better left in the past.

I could tell by the look on her face that she went there too, and trust me, 'there' is far from a happy place for us. Right now I saw two choices. We could excuse ourselves from the reception, go someplace private and talk about it, or we could stay here and dance.

The DJ made the decision for me when he broke out some old school rap. It would have been sacrilege to walk out on Rob Base and EZ Rock's It Takes Two To Make A Thing Go Right.

Five songs later, we were worn out and headed back to our table. I knew Jenisse didn't want to have the talk we should have had ten years ago. Instead of pushing the issue, I left and returned with a drink.

She swallowed half the cranberry juice with ginger ale in a long pull before the glass hit the table.

"Thanks Jay." She finished it with a second long swallow. "Not just for the drink, but for bringing me here. I know you probably have better things to do than babysit me."

I didn't, but I wouldn't let her know. Instead, I flashed my megawatt smile.

"You're welcome. You know I couldn't let you show up to your college roommate's wedding looking like you can't get a man."

Jenisse side-eyed me, glanced the other way for a second then and simultaneously wiggled her butt in the seat while she held on to the hem of her dress. Satisfied with her adjustments, she looked back at me.

"I'm getting a bad case of BWBB- Black Woman's Big Booty. Maybe that's why the men are scarce these days."

She had the nerve to slap her thigh, which caused me to look there by reflex- and enjoy the view by nature.

"Do you think I need to lose weight?"

There was only one way to handle that kind of question, and I jumped in without hesitation. "You sure do! What you weighing these days, four fifty? Five hundred pounds? You are *huge!*"

The side-eye transformed into a full-on death glare, and this shoulder-punch was a lot less girly. Guess I hit a sore spot. She sure did on me.

"Jeremiah…"

"Oh, like I'm supposed to be skurred because you used my full name.

Idiot that I was, I messed around and took another look. Jenisse was down a good hundred pounds from when I first met her, and carried what's left extremely well. Instead of overweight, she was Serena Williams fine.

"Did you really think I'd answer that? I may not be a genius, but I do know that no man in his right mind should ever answer a question about a woman's weight."

"I'm not trying to pick a fight!" Jenisse fiddled with the tiny blue purse on the table between us. "I honestly need to know if you think I need to lose weight."

"I don't think you have any more you can lose. Lately, you've lost the same five pounds about twenty-nine times. That should tell you something. You look fine. I'm proud of you for losing so much weight when your health was at risk, and especially for keeping it off. Trust me, you're looking good. Matter of fact, I'm about to go hurt that dude over there if he keeps looking at my date."

Jenisse almost choked on her drink when she saw where I was looking. The bride's eighty-nine-year-old grandfather stared with longing, as if remembering a time when he kept company with women like her.

"You wrong for that!"

Before I could reply, Jenisse said she wanted to dance again. We hit the floor just in time for some slow jams, starting with Love Takes Time. How appropriate.

Slow dancing reminded me all too well that we're close in height, and with two-inch heels on, she looked me in the eye. It was murder on my self-control when her body fit mine so perfectly, especially when she kissed me by mistake. She wasn't trying to make a move; she noticed Fantasy Man and one of the bridesmaids getting their slow drag on and almost broke her neck when she whipped her head around to get a better look. When she did that, her lips dragged across mine. I didn't mind, but if she ever kissed me again, I need it to be on purpose.

The DJ chose that moment to switch to Luther Vandross. If Only For One Night was the last song the two of us needed to hear. I looked at Jenisse, she looked at me and we walked off the dance floor without a word.

I didn't have to ask her if she was ready to go. That song killed any further desire we had for fun. I followed her as she said her goodbyes to her friends and we headed out. I dropped Jenisse off at her front door, we did our usual awkward good night shuffle and I headed home. I wasn't in the house more than ten minutes before my cell rang.

I answered on the first ring.

"Jeremiah! You're home. I--."

She barely choked back a sob. Something's wrong here. There's a picture of Mama CC in the dictionary next to 'strong black woman' in the dictionary and she's on the other end of the phone trying to hold back tears. This from a woman who not only survived the worst life had to offer without flinching, but turned around and paid it forward.

"It's Erik."

I jerked my head up. "Did something happen to him?"

"I wouldn't know if something did."

I got it. My jackass brother Erik, Mama CC's only biological child out of all of us she's taken in over the years still wasn't talking to her.

"Mama? What happened?"

Another sob almost escaped. "Some of the Missionaries and I- -sat with Sister Clemington earlier. From church."

Her pause was like a black hole that sucked in every bit of my attention.

"Her son died today."

Those words hit me like a stomach punch. Brother Clemington just lost his year-long fight with pancreatic cancer. He was ten years younger than me. Twenty-eight year olds aren't supposed to die, from cancer or anything else.

"She was with him every d-day. Praying over him when he was asleep, talking with him when he was awake, holding his hand..."

Her voice broke. I didn't mind. I don't think I could have said anything right that minute if I wanted to.

"H-her son- - her son is gone, but she was with him. The whole time, she was with him, from the day he was diagnosed until this morning when G-god called him home. It's the worst nightmare a parent can have, but at least she was there for him."

Another gut punch.

"You do a good job of keeping me up on how Erik is, but I still miss him. Anything could be going on in his life and unless you find out, I wouldn't know. He just won't talk to us."

She completely lost it, and that almost took me with her.

"Mama, I'll talk to him again. I can get him to come around, I know it. He's hardheaded, but he still loves you. I know he does."

I heard her trying to compose herself.

"Jay, thank you for listening. I needed this. And thank you for offering to talk to him"

We talked a few more minutes before we disconnected. She sounded a lot better, if she hadn't, I would have been over there in a hot minute.

I guess she's allowed to have a moment just like everybody else. This just wasn't fair. Mama CC had fifteen of us she's mentored (and halfway raised) over the years, but the only one she actually gave birth to was the one who caused her all the problems. Let me call this boy and see what's up.

Both Erik's cell and landline rang about ten times each and went to voicemail. I was tempted to go over there and beat the snot out of him for what he was putting his mother through.

A text came through just as I laid my phone aside. The call from Mama CC's had unnerved me, but this text from one of my sisters was terrifying!

RU STLL GUD 4 NXT STRDY? WE'LL B THR @ 6.

2

"Uncle J! He hit me again!"

I separated the same niece and nephew for the three hundred forty-seventh time while trying to keep track of the other kids in my peripheral vision. Each time, I questioned my sanity for agreeing to watch six kids under the age of seven overnight.

I had to laugh at the irony of God's sense of humor. I'd been praying for marriage and children. Last weekend I took Jenisse to that wedding and now I'm up to my butt in children.

Time for the secret weapon; the bag of DVDs the happy parents sent along with their assorted offspring.

"Okay, what are we watching first?"

To my complete surprise, they agreed on one without much argument. Right when they got hypnotized by an animated snowman, a mountain man and reindeer battling winter elements and mythical assorted mythical characters, my phone rang. My mistake was trying to keep one eye on the kids while I went to get it. My punishment was that I whacked my knee on the edge of the desk.

I managed to redirect any free-form cursing into unintelligible angry mumbling. No sense teaching the kids any words their mothers would come get me for.

"Hello?"

The warm chuckle on the other end of the phone instantly dispelled my anger and most of the pain.

"Now I know your mama didn't teach you to answer the phone like that!"

"You should know; you raised me about as much as she did!"

Mama CC laughed out loud. "Okay smarty, don't make me come over there. You're never too old for a whipping!"

We both laughed knowing good and well that even if she was inclined to take a belt to me, she wasn't going to jump on a plane back home to do it. She flew to Cincinnati yesterday morning to oversee the creation of yet another branch of her expanding business entity.

Lydia Enterprises was on the rise, and battered women everywhere were thankful for its success. Mama CC had a gift for not only rescuing women from bad situations, but also provided them with job skills. As prosperous as it was, Mama CC sounded like she was glad to be about ten states removed from all this.

"Actually I busted my knee on the desk trying to get to the phone. Believe me, you don't sound too chipper when that happens."

"And why were you rushing so hard to get the phone? Got a hot date lined up?"

"Yeah, right! What I got is six kids in here watching a movie. The only woman I expect tonight is the female police officer who comes to investigate the noise complaint."

Mama CC couldn't hide her laughter. "You're the one who lost his mind and took six kids at the same time. If the police do come, they'll probably book you for temporary insanity."

"True, but what else could I do? Deb had surgery, Ruth is taking care of her and you ran away from home. Who else could they depend on?"

"What's Jenisse doing this weekend? I'm surprised you didn't enlist her to help you with the Mongol hordes."

"She worked a ton of overtime this week. I don't want to bother her unless it's an absolute emergency."

"Hmmph. Given the fact that you've taken her to two weddings and a formal dance in the past two months, she should have volunteered to help you out. She's still using you as ego defense."

"Ma'am?"

"Jenisse feels like she can't go to events like that without a man on her arm. She's defending her ego by dragging you around instead of letting you be free to get your own dates now and again."

"Get my own date? She's the only woman I've been out with lately. Apparently she's the only one willing to be seen in public with me."

"It can't be that bad, now. You're a handsome young man with a lot to offer and you mean to tell me you can't get a respectable woman to go out with you?"

"Most of the respectable women are already married or spoken for.

The ones who are left apparently want someone looking less like JJ from Good Times and more like Idris Elba."

"Boy, if you don't stop putting yourself down... You are *not* unattractive; I don't know why you seem to think you are."

I couldn't even defend myself on that before she cut me off.

"I know you have your hands full, so I won't keep you. I just wanted to check on you." Mama CC couldn't stifle a laugh. "I'll be praying for you."

As soon as she hung up, I whipped my head around to see what the kids were doing. To my complete surprise, they were still mesmerized by the movie and hadn't moved a muscle.

I then checked the bassinet to make sure the baby was still asleep. I prayed that he was. Prayer answered; he was out cold and I hoped he stayed that way until his mama claimed him.

I looked around at all the children in my house. It made me think of Mama CC. I was the first one she reached out to. She got most of us during her time as President of Student Affairs at the University of Delaware. She and Mr. Thurman never hesitated; when they saw someone like me who needed them, they reached right out. They and Erik never made any of us feel less than welcome, even when some of us had to live with them off and on for different reasons. I owed them more than I could ever repay. I mean, I lost my whole family, but God sent me another one. That's why I took six kids at once, and why I did so much else for my siblings. All we had was each other, and I won't let any of them down.

Two hours into Kid Fest and I was still in one piece. Frozen calmed the savage beasts down like nobody's business. It took a snack and about a million interactive games on PBSkids.com to keep them calm enough to put on another movie.

Wreck-It-Ralph got them pretty zoned out. I might just survive this experience after all.

A diaper change quieted the baby. I placed him on my shoulder and walked the floor until he fell asleep.

As soon as I thought I was safe, the doorbell rang and woke him back up. Now I had to juggle him so I could find out who in the world was trying to mess up my flow.

I opened the door just a crack and two tiny tornadoes in matching pink and green outfits pushed it all the way open and blew past me.

"Uncle Jay! Uncle Jay!"

Three of my five senses engaged at the same time. I felt Carmen and Angie grip my legs with such force that they almost took me down. I heard an engine rev hard and *saw* the backside of my brother Joel's car as he sped away from the curb at warp speed. The car *I* paid to get back from the repo man.

Carmen held up her treasured Doc McStuffins backpack. "Daddy said 'cause all the other kids are here, he'd let us come too and stay all night!"

I could only imagine the look on my face; it probably matched the look on the baby's face when Thing One and Thing Two tried to snatch him out of my arms. I saved his life by shooing them into the den with the other kids, but nothing was gonna save me now. Not when Queen Carmen The First would no doubt start ordering her cousins around any second and Princess Angie would co-sign. It was about to be World War III up in here.

I walked the room trying to get the baby to fall back to sleep. Somewhere around the third baby-slap upside my head, it occurred to me that it was time to call for backup.

I played my ace in the hole and stood by the door and waited. When Jenisse arrived, she took one look around and laughed in my face. "Your reinforcement is here, Jay. You can relax now."

Jenisse looked nauseatingly fresh in a pink sweatshirt and new blue jeans. I'm pretty sure I could be the poster boy for 'Disheveled' right about now.

I couldn't blame her for laughing at the sheer chaos she walked into. I had the baby screaming in my ear, toddlers holding my legs so tight to that my sweatpants were coming down. The boy on my left leg complained about Carmen having turned off their movie to watch the Disney Channel and the girl on the right leg was suddenly consumed with the fact that she didn't know where her mommy was. People all over Delaware probably heard the verbal equivalent of the Trojan War that took place the family room between the Terrorist Twins and the kids who weren't attached to my shins.

Jenisse put her overnight bag on the floor beside the door and pried the two toddlers off my legs. They transferred their anaconda grips to her neck in greeting. "Uh, Jay? I hate to ask, but what's that on your shirt?"

"That would be the juice boxes I gave Carmen and Angie. Instead of drinking them, they decided to use them as Super Soakers on me."

Jenisse put the Death Grip Kids on the floor, rolled up her sleeves and sighed. "Men. Since you look like you won't last another two minutes, I'm going to pull the plug on this madness. Keep doing what you were doing with the original six and let me lay hands on the Demonettes."

I had to laugh as she took the toddlers with her and waded into the melee. On paper she just signed on for an unfair division of labor in her favor, but the reality was, I got the easier end of the bargain. Joel's girls were the equal of any ten children alive. Fortunately for me, those girls adored Jenisse; their own momma (and the belt she kept in her purse) couldn't get those little heathens to behave as easily as Jenisse could.

A chorus of small voices rang out. "Auntie 'Niece!"

The ensuing silence was sudden and downright deafening. Just like that, the verbal chaos ended. Two seconds later, Jenisse came out with a little terrorist holding each hand and the Death Grip Kids following them.

"I put the movie back on for the kids who wanted to finish it. These two are with me. If the other girls want to join us for girls' time, they can. The fellas are yours."

Carmen and Angie followed Jenisse without a word, and the other kids ran off to watch the resumed movie

I never thought this house would know peace again. And right on cue, the baby ended his voluntary insomnia and passed out on my shoulder.

If I live to be a hundred, I'd never understand how her mere presence did that.

And Joel wouldn't live to see his next birthday by the time I got through with him.

3

I woke up at six in the morning to dead silence. I wasn't sure if that was a good thing since Joel's girls were part ninja. They could be skulking around the house plotting against me and I'd never know it until it was too late.

I put my own ninja skills to the test, slipped out of bed as quietly as I could and did a fast recon. Child-filled sleeping bags were scattered around my living room like land mines. In the far corner, Jenisse dozed on the pull-out couch, covered by the blanket I gave her and two adoring little girls. For a moment I forgot all the mayhem from last night and enjoyed the sight of the woman I've loved since college snuggled up with the Demonettes. They looked so peaceful when they weren't planning world domination.

I shook my head to break the spell and slipped into the bathroom. Since I knew that the silence wouldn't last much longer, I showered, dressed and took advantage of the lull in the action to go online and check my finances.

My investments were doing well enough. I'd been faithful in putting money in my savings account. It only took a minute to balance my checking account and credit card statements.

My brothers and sisters ragged me about being cheap. I'm not. I just knew that I had to make what I had last. I did because what was placed in my hands was the result of more tragedy than anyone should ever have to go through. I received this money and property from the deaths of my parents, my grandparents and my aunt and uncle. I could live off my inheritance if I wanted to, but I chose to work.

I also worked at growing what was in my hand to be an example to my siblings. As hard as I tried to be strong in that area, I had to admit that my family was my weakness. Every time one of them asks for financial help I give it. Over the years, their hands have been out so much that I opened a third account just for their constant loan requests.

In a sense, I didn't mind; they're all the family I have in this world. I was an only child before I lost everybody. God sent me a second family through Mama CC and Mr. Thurman. None of us were easy to deal with; we all had issues.

I was the first one they found, and given how bad a shape I was in, I owed it to the Dawsons to help them help the others. As dedicated I am to helping, their constant requests are getting old; especially since the Bank of Jeremiah only receives occasional repayment. I'm thinking Mama CC was right when she told me that I had become an enabler.

Case in point: Joel. Any other time he would have asked me to loan him some money. This time, that fool took out a car title loan for $500.00. Because he only made minimum payments, his interest skyrocketed. Joel got so far behind that they repossessed his car. I ended up paying over a thousand dollars to dig him out of the hole he was in.

In return he signed a contract to pay me back $150.00 each payday. He's been paid twice since I redeemed his car and I haven't seen a payment yet. I could add that to the $3000.00 he's owed me from about twenty other loans and write it all off, or I could get creative. But before I deal with him repaying me, I need to address the immediate issue; payback for his latest scheme. And I just figured out what to do first.

I put my financial stuff aside, tiptoed into the living room and reached for the wallet and car keys I left on the coffee table. Jenisse awakened with a smile, but held still in deference to the girls' blissful slumber.

"Hold down the fort for a few minutes. I need to make a run."

I hoped she heard me; in trying not to wake up the girls, I whispered so low dogs probably couldn't catch it. She nodded as if she understood me, and I slipped out to put project 'Trifling Little Brother' into action.

"*Answer* this phone, Joel!"

I'm about to throw this phone through his window if he doesn't answer.

When his voicemail came on, I screamed a message onto his voicemail. "I *know* you're there and I *know* you're screening your calls. You got five minutes to get your raggedy, dropping-people-off-with-no-warning butt outta bed and get your kids."

I disconnected the call and walked back to my car. Jenisse had gotten out; she leaned against the passenger door laughing her butt off.

To my surprise, Carmen and Angie hadn't broken or tried to steal my car in the short time I'd left them alone. I answered their questioning looks.

"Your daddy just woke up. He'll be down to let you in soon."

As if on cue, Joel's wife Barbara came outside. When I paroled the girls from the car seats I keep on hand, they swarmed to hug their mother before they diverted to the front yard and the toys they'd left all over the lawn.

I let them run free, headed for the front door, stepped inside and raised my voice to the rafters. "Joel! Get your butt down here!"

Silence. Well, except for Jenisse and Barbara snickering. They must have sneaked in behind me while I was screaming.

"Don't *make* me embarrass you in front of your wife! I'll come up there and smack your name clean off the public record!"

As Jenisse and Barbara burst out laughing I heard shuffling from upstairs. Joel will be down soon.

I gave Jenisse a big hug, and held it a bit longer than necessary. "Nothing I say can thank you enough for coming over to help me with the babysitting. Since words won't cut it, I hope my actions will."

I removed ten crisp twenty-dollar bills from my wallet, liberated from the ATM when I went out earlier. I counted them and handed them to Jenisse.

"Barbara looks a bit stressed out, what with having such, um, energetic children and a husband like Joel to deal with. I think she could use a little down time."

Jenisse happily took the money and rewarded me with an all too satisfying hug and kiss on the cheek. "I totally agree. That's why we're going to have a Girls Day out. Thanks, Jay."

I smiled. "And how long do you think this Girls Day Out might last?"

Jenisse pondered for a moment. "It's hard to say. We could be out until well past 8:00 tonight."

Barbara laughed out loud. 8:00 was the girls' bedtime and the whole family knew it.

"That long?" I scratched my head as if confused. "What a coincidence. Since Mama CC's out of town. Me and Mr. Thurman are gonna try to get tickets to the Hampton/Delaware State football game in Dover. If we score, we won't be back until at least that late ourselves."

Jenisse couldn't hold back a smile. "Isn't that the game Joel tried to get tickets for?"

Barbara nodded. "He *did* get tickets."

I pointed to Carmen and Angie, who zipped around the lawn like hummingbirds on crack. "Somehow I don't think he'll make it."

A smile crossed Barbara's lips. "I think I'd have to agree with that assessment."

The two of them went to check on the girls. Out of the corner of my eye, I spied the coveted football tickets on the entry hall table. Without a bit of remorse, I slipped them into my back pocket.

He won't be needing these today.

I joined the ladies outside and watched the energetic duo.

Carmen and Angie had found a jump rope. Carmen went first, and whipped the rope over her head with such force she nearly generated a hurricane. When Angie had her turn, she windmilled so hard she almost stomped herself into the earth's core.

Barbara looked at her daughters. "What did you feed them?"

My attempt to appear innocent failed. "Nothing out of the ordinary. They had Froot Loops, French toast with syrup and hot chocolate to drink."

I retrieved a half-filled Starbucks cup and handed it to Barbara. "Want some espresso? I have some left and I know how much you like it."

Barbara's eyes widened. "You didn't."

"The hot chocolate needed some flavoring."

Barbara failed to contain a laugh and shook her head. "Lawd, he done drugged my babies. Now I know we're staying out past eight tonight."

As Joel stumbled outside clad in a marginally clean T-shirt and pair of jeans, Barbara got down on one knee and beckoned to Carmen and Angie.

"Girls! Mommy's going out with Auntie 'Niece today. You get to spend all day with Daddy. Won't that be fun?"

The Flash and the Road Runner roared their approval and paused long enough to hug their mother, me and Jenisse before they turned the full force of their chemically enhanced conversational skills on their father. They chattered away like magpies, barely pausing for breath as they tag-team shared every detail of their time with Uncle Jay.

Joel started to mumble his thanks to me for keeping them when a moment of dawning comprehension hit him.

Barbara kissed him on the cheek, bid him a cheerful farewell and slid into Joel and Barbara's car with Jenisse before he could say a word.

I clapped him on the back. "Enjoy your children bruh; they'll be grown before you know it. When you look back, you'll treasure these times you had to spend with them."

I waved the tickets over my head." Thanks for the tickets. Mr. Thurman and I will have a good time."

I laughed like a mad scientist in a horror movie as I got into my car and pulled off.

4

"**A**re you a man?"

"Sir?"

"You heard me. Are. You. A. Man?"

This was such a good day. DelState won the football game, and Mr. Thurman and I decided to get a bite to eat and let the traffic die down before heading home. I was enjoying myself until the ambush.

I glanced down at my crotch. "Last time I checked. Why do you ask?"

Mr. Thurman's patented narrow-eyed death stare fell somewhere between 'I know I raised you better than this' and 'you idiot'. That meant that trying to deflect his words with humor wouldn't work. Last time I saw that expression was when he and I had to get Joel out of jail.

He put his fork down and kept his gaze locked on me. "You've been our son since college. What's that, twenty years now?"

"Give or take a year."

"Jeremiah, for as long as I've known you, you and Jenisse have been joined at the hip, and it stopped being a healthy give-and-take relationship about a month or so after you two met."

If someone had a gun to my head, I wouldn't have been able to answer. The Incident happened maybe two months into our relationship; can't get much unhealthier than that.

"You've been in love with her from the beginning. I suspect that the feeling is mutual, but she's got so many issues she doesn't know who she is, much less how to recognize the right man for her."

This man was determined to break me down and all I could do was let him.

"Jeremiah, does CC run me?"

My eyes got wide, and Mr. Thurman laughed.

"This is not a trick question. Do I do everything your mama says without question? Do I let her disregard my feelings or disrespect me in any way without calling her on it?"

"No, can't say I've ever seen that."

"And you never will. CC won't have it, and neither will I. We've been together thirty-four years. We've made it this far because we don't just love each other, we like each other. Because we like each other, we respect each other."

Another bull's-eye. I started to feel like an emotional dart board.

"How about you, son? Do you and Jenisse have it like that?"

Oh great. *Now* he lets me talk. I had no idea what to say.

"Let me make it easy on you. You don't. You let Jenisse abuse you every day, and not only don't you call her on it, you aid and abet."

Deep breath. Don't get huffy with your old man- that's never a good look. "Hold up. You make it sound like she pimp-slaps me for dinner and cusses me out for dessert. You *know* I don't roll like that."

Mr. Thurman took a sip of his coffee. "Maybe you don't let her abuse you physically, but you let her run you. She's made it clear she won't date you, yet you act like her boyfriend anyway. You take her to every social event she wants to attend, unless she's seeing someone, in which case she goes incog-Negro on you. If her car breaks down, she's calling you first. If a light bulb burns out in her house, she has you there before the light fades. You're always there when she needs you. Can you say the same about her?"

My lips tightened. He's right.

"I'm there for *everybody.* That's what the oldest is supposed to do; look out for the younger ones."

Mr. Thurman didn't flinch. "We'll get to them in a minute. But now that you mention it, when was the last time you took Deborah to a wedding? Or mowed Ruth's lawn?"

Touché.

"And while we're on the subject, you can look out for your brothers and sisters without enabling them."

"Enabling them?"

"You are at their beck and call, 24-7. Every time I look around, you're doing for one or another of them. Don't think I don't know they all come to you when they need a "loan" and your mother and I won't give it. They probably go to you first now. Anybody pay you back yet?"

I side-eyed him. "Erik did."

"He's the only one. Tell me I'm lying."

Silence.

"I know I'm right. I'm pretty sure Joel has never paid you back. If he has, tell me how that feels, because *I* sure don't know."

I had to laugh.

"And how's that car loan coming?"

I felt the need to explain myself. "The only reason I paid to get Joel's car off the repo lot is so he'd stop asking to borrow mine all the time. Besides, a man with a wife and two kids needs a car."

"Let me guess. He hasn't paid you anything yet."

I nodded

"How's he going to learn to take care of his family if you keep bailing him out?"

I nodded again.

Mr. Thurman leaned in a bit and drilled me with a hard glare. "There's more. You're both the family ATM and King Babysitter. The ones with kids leave their little people with you like your name's Cliff Huxtable."

My lips tightened even more. I hoped I wasn't glaring at Mr. Thurman. It wouldn't be cool to be rude to someone who was trying to help. I took a minute before I could find my voice and respond. "You of all people should know that parents need a break from their kids sometimes."

"Of course they do. But as usual, you take it too far. I guarantee you, none of your brothers and sisters get asked to watch six kids at the same time alone, because all the others would tell the one asking where they could go and the best route to get there. Joel knew he could get away with his little stunt because he knows you're a soft touch."

"If I was that soft, he'd be here with you instead of alone with his sugared-up little heathens.

Mr. Thurman smiled. "True. Not to belabor the point, but you take more crap from your siblings than I thought was humanly possible."

"Oh, I'm not through with Joel."

I told him my plans for when (not if) Joel missed his third consecutive payment. As I talked, Mr. Thurman's eyes widened. Without warning, he burst out laughing and couldn't stop for a few minutes.

I chucked. "Oh look, it's after 8:00. Since I'm pretty sure Jenisse and Barbara are still out on the town, that means Joel will have to put his little darlings to bed all by himself."

Mr. Thurman managed to bring his laughter down to a chuckle. "If they haven't killed him by now."

An image of Joel hogtied with an apple in his mouth and his daughters running around the house wreaking havoc popped into my head.

Mr. Thurman broke into my thoughts. "It's good to know you *do* have a backbone. Make sure you keep it when you deal with Jenisse, 'because something has to change. You're the only one who can change it."

We paid our bill and left. I slid in behind the wheel and headed for home.

"One more point to consider. You're a good man with a lot to offer the right woman. Jenisse may not be the right woman."

Mr. Thurman put his head back for a nap, leaving me to drive home on automatic pilot.

I processed everything Mr. Thurman told me as I drove. His last statement echoed through my head. Funny. Jenisse had been the only woman in my heart for so long that I didn't know if I could consider anyone else. Might be fun to try though.

5

Food shopping would be a lot easier if it was just for me.

Thing is, six of my fifteen siblings, live here in Delaware. That meant that after Mama CC's, my house was Kid Central. As often as the kids are there, I have to keep juice boxes and other stuff they like on hand.

I checked my mental grocery list. Cookie supply was running low. I should grab some of those oatmeal ones all the kids like those.

I turned to get the cookies and saw something much sweeter walk past.

Whoa. That woman was gorgeous! Soft brown eyes, flawless golden tan complexion, body by Tyra Banks, genuine smile I am TOAST.

Enough of that. I needed to focus on what I came to do.

I finished my shopping them got into the checkout line. Even though I only had a few things, it still seemed like it took me forever to check out and leave.

As I cleared the supermarket door, something caught my eye. The woman I saw earlier was about five feet ahead of me, juggling two grocery bags and her purse as she headed for her car. The juggling act got a bit complicated. She got her bags under control, but her purse hit the ground, and something slipped out of her hand at the same time. She grabbed her purse, straightened up and headed for her car without realizing she'd lost anything. As I got closer to where she'd just been, a glint of color snagged my attention. I followed it to a cell phone in an eye-catching case: royal blue with gold trim. I switched my bag to my left hand and scooped up the phone with my right.

"Miss! Excuse me, Miss!"

She turned to face me. I chuckled when I saw her hand meander toward her purse. I kept my distance, just in case she pulled out some pepper spray on me. Or worse for all I know, she could have a gun in there. "Yes, what can I do for you?"

Between her eyes and the sound of her voice, I darn near forgot my own name. Somehow I managed to activate my voice and held out her missing item where she could see it. "Uh, you, uh, dropped your phone."

Her smile outshone the sun and the trace of "what does this fool want?" dropped from her demeanor. "Thank you! I didn't even realize I'd dropped it."

"Well, you did have a few things keeping you busy."

Her giggle sounded like sweet music. I handed her the phone; her hand brushed mine as she took it from me, and darn if I didn't feel something. A cynic would say it was static electricity, but static never made my heart race.

I indicated the cover. "Let me guess. Sigma Gamma Rho?"

She laughed. "What gave it away?"

"The gold trim. Otherwise I might've thought you're just really into blue."

"It does stand out in a crowd."

We laughed again.

"Seriously though, thanks for finding my phone. I would've been all the way home not realizing I'd lost it."

She cocked her head slightly, as if trying to see all the way through me. She was about four inches shorter than I am, which made her tilt her head up to look me in the eye. "I'm Symone Donovan by the way. I recognize you from church, but I don't know your name."

I felt my face stretch to ungodly proportions, and couldn't respond until Goofy Grin vanished.

"I knew you looked familiar, but I couldn't place where I knew you from. I'm Jeremiah McAllister."

We chatted a few more minutes and then my phone rang.

Symone chuckled. "I'll leave you in peace to get that. It was nice officially meeting you, and thanks again for finding my phone!"

"You too. Guess I'll see you in church?"

She waved and slid into her car. My phone blared again and shattered all remnants of the peaceful conversation I'd just shared with Symone. I looked down at the display and wasn't the least bit surprised to see who it was.

"Hey Jenisse."

"Are we still on for lunch?"

"Are you still buying?"

She laughed. "Yes El Cheapo, I'm buying. After you had to deal with Babysitting From Hell over the weekend, it's the least I can do.

"'El Cheapo?' Who usually buys?"

We bantered back and forth for a few more minutes before disconnecting.

It took me three hours longer than expected, but I finally got back home. After the supermarket, I stopped past home to drop off my groceries, met Jenisse for lunch as planned, dropped her off at her job and stopped by my own job to pick up something. I figured that was enough running around for my day off, but my car figured otherwise. That joker died on me right in front of work.

It wasn't a problem getting AAA out here to tow me to the mechanic, but getting someone to come get me from there? You'd think I had leprosy, shingles, the flu and Ebola all at once the way these ninjas avoided my calls. Fortunately, there was one I could always count on. He not only answered on the first ring, but he came right over here to get me.

"Thanks for giving me a ride home, Erik I really appreciate it."

"No problem Jay; glad I was around. What's up with your hoopty now?"

I had to laugh. Only Erik would call my Lexus a hoopty.

"It wouldn't start, and wouldn't take a jump either. I hope it just needs a new battery. If mechanics have to go into the ignition system, they start planning college for their kids and booking cruises for their wives."

"Got that right. Hey, why didn't Jenisse come get you? DigiBank is right across the pavilion from where you work."

"I couldn't catch up to her."

Erik rolled his eyes. "Uh huh. Let me guess. When it was time for you two to go to lunch earlier, she blew up your phone. Now when you need her help, your butt is stranded."

We pulled up at my house. I invited Erik inside so we could talk over a couple of sodas. I told him about meeting Symone. Erik blinked, snorted and nearly fell off the couch laughing.

"Hold up. You actually talked to a woman who's not part of the family? And she just happens to be a member of Calvary UAC, but not one you know well. Yet."

Oh great, the midget matchmaker is in full effect. At five four Erik's the shortest in the family, but he comes off huge when it comes to minding my business, especially in terms of my love life.

"Give it a rest. I can't even figure out Jenisse, much less work out what to say to someone like Symone."

I took a pull off my Dr. Pepper and changed the subject. "Maybe you can answer a question for me."

Erik took a deep swallow of his own. "What?"

"Why does your mother have to ask me how you're doing? Is there a special reason why you're still not talking to her?"

Erik didn't meet my eyes. "It's complicated.

"This ain't a Facebook relationship status. How tough is it to sit down and talk to your own mother? It's been almost a year!"

"It's not as easy as you make it sound." Erik sighed. "It's, well, sometimes it seems like she doesn't really care what's going on with me. There were lots of times when I needed some advice or what have you and she had better things to do than to give it to me."

"You gotta be kidding me! Your mom lives to tell folks what she thinks they should do! That's probably why I took to her so fast when she met me. I was eighteen and having to make decisions my parents should have been making for me. Why wouldn't she want to do that for you?"

"Let's just say she didn't always have the time to get to me. You know Mom stays busy, and I suppose I couldn't schedule my crises at a convenient time."

I decided not to push any further for now and changed the subject, again. "I have another question for you. Why is it that thin women always think they're fat and the ones who do weigh four hundred pounds walk around wearing halter tops and biker shorts?"

Erik nearly snorted soda out his nose. "Let me guess. Jenisse needed affirmation about her weight again."

"Dag dude, no manners. Don't be spitting in my house. Anyway, you know how that goes. We went to lunch today and we hadn't even ordered yet before she hit me with it again. It never ceases to amaze me how she can keep a straight face while asking me the question that's gotten so many men verbally dissected over the centuries. 'Do I need to lose weight?' Erik, me answering that question is dangerous on two levels. Besides the obvious, she's inviting me to look her up and down to make an evaluation, and I don't want to go there. Staring at her body like that takes me places I don't want to go."

When he finally managed to stop laughing he shared his thoughts.

"I feel you on that, man. You've been into her since college; it's hard to just turn it off."

He paused. "But, maybe it's time you gave it a real try. She might be your dream woman, but she's not the only woman out there who might like you. When was the last time you went out with anyone not named Jenisse?"

I hesitated.

"That's what I thought."

"Have you been talking to your dad about this? He said something real similar when we went to the football game Saturday."

Erik shrugged. "Hey, he's a smart guy. You might want to think about it."

"And you might want to think about talking to your mama. I'm getting sick of making excuses for you."

We talked a few more minutes, I threatened to whoop his tail if he didn't talk to his mom and he left unwhooped, talking some noise about having a date to get ready for.

Brothers. Sometimes I felt like I was better off when I was an only child.

Hmmm. This time spent with Erik was almost normal. He still won't deal with his folks, but he was there when I needed him and he didn't ask me for any money. Why couldn't it be like this with the rest of the family?

Because I wouldn't let it.

That had to change.

6

"My brethren, count it all joy when you fall into various trials, knowing that the testing of your faith produces patience. But let patience have its perfect work, that you may be perfect and complete, lacking nothing. If any of you lacks wisdom, let him ask of God, who gives to all liberally and without reproach, and it will be given to him." James 1:2-5

Gotta love this Bible app. Beats carrying a Bible around everywhere I go and then losing it somewhere.

I read the passage again, and something clicked inside me. My whole life was tied up in other folks, specifically my family. That crew kept me busy, and I needed more.

Maybe working out had me all pumped up, but I'm through with all this. I've propped my family up for so long I have no life of my own.

I'm sick of being the family ATM. I never should have let it get this far, but since I did, I needed to do something to stop it. Joel's first in line. Another payday passed and he was MIA as usual. He was about to find out why you really ought to read the fine print when you sign something.

I'm also tired of waiting for Jenisse to see me as anything but her big brother, but I'm not meeting any other women worth my time. Of course that could have something to do with the fact that I don't really go anywhere to meet women not named Jenisse.

I wonder if Symone would be interested in going out with me.

The door to the women's locker room flew open. I heard the laughter before I saw them, and almost dropped my phone when I saw Symone come out behind Jenisse. Talk about a pleasant surprise.

"Hi Jeremiah! Long time no see."

"Symone, you consider last Sunday at church a long time? How've you been?"

"Can't complain. Amazing who you run into in the shower though."

Jenisse narrowed her eyes. "That really didn't come out right."

"Anyway. I saw you two working out, but I figured I'd leave you to sweat in peace. I know I don't like it when someone interrupts my workout flow."

As we moved past the workout area toward the exit, two dudes to my right almost dropped their weights and a third guy almost fell off the treadmill trying to turn and get a better look. Sad.

"Not a problem I've ever had, so I'll take you ladies' word for it."

Couldn't say I blamed them for staring. Jenisse and Symone standing side by side was a lot like Serena Williams hanging with Janelle Monae. That's a whole lot of fine in one place.

You'd thought Symone was fully made up and dressed to the nines for all the attention she was getting. I guess to those thirsty looking dudes, jeans and a Sigma Gamma Rho sweatshirt looked just as good on her as an evening gown would.

Hmmm. Evening gown. Maybe I should ask her to the next formal instead of Jenisse.

"Symone, is this one of your regular times to come here? I haven't seen you here before."

Her smile alone was murder on my self-control; I wouldn't allow myself to think about her body.

"I do come on Saturdays, but I'm usually here a little later. I came in earlier today because I have errands to run."

Her words could be my in. I nodded in Jenisse's direction. "That's good to know. Sometimes I have to travel on business and when I'm not here, it'd be nice if this one had someone to work out with so she doesn't get lazy."

I dodged the swat Jenisse aimed at my head.

Symone laughed. "You sound like my brother. But if you're asking me to join you guys for workouts, I'd love to. It gets boring sometimes coming alone. My brother comes with me when he can, but you know cops have strange hours. And if I'm here with somebody, it reduces the odds of some weirdo trying to get my phone number."

Good. Score one for Operation Get A Date.

"So, what are you two up to now?"

I couldn't stop from rolling my eyes. "We're about to go where no man should have to go, shopping!"

Jenisse laughed. "We have a ton of nieces and nephews to shop for. Me and Jay prefer doing our Christmas shopping now instead of getting into December when the Christmas feeding frenzy happens."

Symone's whole face lit up, "Wow, I was about to do the same thing for my little cousins. Mind if I join you?"

Score two for Operation Get A Date.

We followed Symone to her house so she could drop off her car. As soon as she was out of earshot, I turned to Jenisse. "I didn't know you knew Symone."

Jenisse chuckled. "We just really met. I started hanging out with the Singles Ministry and she's the Vice President or Secretary or something. I like her she's good company and she knows how to help folks handle being single. I didn't know you knew her either."

I told her about running into Symone at the store.

"I bet she thought you were some crazy man trying to pick her up."

"All I picked up was her phone!"

We laughed until Symone came out. Once she was settled into the back seat of my car, we went off to ravage Toys R Us.

The doorbell ruined a great nap. I almost ignored it, but changed my mind and forced myself to answer. When I opened the door, Erik stood there cheesing like the Kool Aid Man.

"Sorry, no salesmen allowed here. Move along."

Erik's eyes rolled upward as he pushed past me. I returned to my comfort zone on the couch and put my head back.

"Jay, where you been? I've been calling you all day."

I opened one eye so I wouldn't go to sleep. "Erik, if you value your life, *never* hang out with two women for whom Extreme Shopping is an Olympic event."

"Uh oh. Who got you? Jenisse and who else?"

"We ran into Symone at Planet Fitness and invited her to come with us to Christmas shop for the kids. I forgot how many other stores there were near Toys R Us."

"Let me guess. When it comes to shopping, Symone is Jenisse's twin separated at birth."

I opened the other eye. "In this family anything's possible. I shoulda known we weren't just buying toys. After the toy store, it took four pairs of shoes, three blouses and two purses to get them to even think about slowing down. I had to bribe them with Ruby Tuesday's to get them out the stores. Thank God they were hungry or I'd still be there holding purses."

Erik cackled like a witch smoking weed.

"Okay Jokey Smurf, you said you were calling me all day. What's going on that you need me to tell yo' mama about instead of just telling her yourself?"

He hesitated.

I came to an upright position. "Oh, this is gonna be good. Give it up, what's the news?"

"This can't go on the family grapevine. It'd cause way too much drama if Mom found out."

"You mean this is worse than when you let Joel hook you up with a blind date and the woman was six foot three?"

He side-eyed me like an expert. "Yeah. That was funny; this is more serious."

Erik paused. "My date the other night? It was Talia."

My eyebrows almost hit my hairline. "Talia? As in the Talia your mom advised you against dating because she's not saved?"

"That's the one."

"Clearly you didn't take her advice. Now I get why you won't talk to Mama CC. You don't want to hear it when, not if, she tells you the same thing all over again."

Erik sighed. "It's not that cut and dried, Jay. I've been interested in Talia since college. You know that. I can't just turn that off any more than you can just suddenly not be interested in Jenisse."

"Okay, I see what you did there. You turned it back on me. All right, I won't tell your mama for now. But, if she asks me straight out if you're seeing Talia, I'm telling her yes."

"Fair enough." Erik stood up to his full height. "Jay, I felt like I wasted a lot of time waiting for Talia to try a relationship with me. Don't make my mistake. Talk to Jenisse again. Tell her your frustrations, your feelings, and your hopes for your relationship. Get it all out in the open, because if you continue to hold it all inside, you will explode. Take it from one who knows."

Erik went home, and left me alone with my thoughts.

What if we talked, I said my piece and she still wouldn't consider me? And why was Symone so heavy on my mind when I'm trying to sort through what I feel about Jenisse?

7

J enisse opened the door of her apartment open so I could follow her inside.

"Have a seat, Jay. Want anything to drink?"

"Water's fine."

She grabbed two cold bottles from her refrigerator, handed me one and sat across from me on the couch.

"Jay, thanks for coming over. I felt like we needed to talk."

"True." I sipped some water. "Lately I've felt like there's a wall between us, and I don't know what we can do to get past it."

"I feel like that too."

Jenisse took a breath. I saw the question in her eyes, and had to force myself to wait for her to say what she needed to say instead of asking it for her.

"I know my issues are driving this. I've been thinking about my mom and my so-called father a lot lately. They put the 'D' in dysfunctional. I mean, all my life he wasn't there except on my birthday and some Christmases, and any time she wasn't letting him spend the night, she was grinning at some other man. I'm sure that that's why I have relationship issues."

She laughed humorlessly. "Jay, how do you know when a man really likes you? I mean, not just interested because he wants some booty, but really wants to be with you?"

This was a subject I knew by heart and now was the time to tell the truth. I set my bottle aside and drew on the courage I'd managed to build.

"Here's a clue. When a man's interested, not just curious, but really falling for you interested you'll know. If nothing else, he'll have a big cheesy grin every time he sees you!"

"You are funny!"

Jenisse's laughter helped me keep going.

"Seriously though, he will. It's nothing a brother can control. If he likes you, as soon as he sees you, the teef pop out."

More sweet laughter.

"When a guy really likes you, you'll know it. Fancy dinners and flowers are easy to do the hard stuff is more subtle. If a guy likes you, he'll invent reasons to talk to you; he'll call or text or find some excuse to come see you. If he knows you're feeling down, he'll do what he can to cheer you up. He'll go shopping with you and hold your purse with minimal complaining. He will extend himself for you in every way."

I paused for effect and then went for the kill. "He'll use taking revenge on his trifling brother as an opportunity to do something nice for you. Because. He. Cares."

Finally got it out there.

Jenisse's eyes widened and then filled with wonder and curiosity. "I thought we were good as brother and sister. Tell me how long you've still been in love with me."

"Doesn't matter. You just told me the truth that I have to accept."

"But I do love you, Jay. It's confusing. I mean, I always liked you from the time I met you. I thought it was just a good friends-play-brother kind of thing until."

I caught myself breathing faster. *Was she finally gonna let me talk about what happened?*

"Twenty years and we've never talked about this. I know, because I usually won't let you. Trust me though Jay, I have never forgotten what happened between us."

I nodded. "It started at the Kappa party with that drunk Jheri curl having dude calling you out."

"He asked me to dance. I said no, and he got an attitude. Called me a fat ho and said nobody wanted me."

"Yup. I was dancing nearby when he said that and I kinda lost it."

"'Kinda lost it?' Jay, you beat him unconscious. I didn't even know you had it in you. It took five guys to pull you off of him."

"He disrespected you. I wasn't having it then, nor would I have it now."

Jenisse blinked. "Wow. Okay, after that I was shaken up. I wanted to leave, and you walked me back to my dorm."

"Your roommate was home that weekend. It wasn't the first time we'd been alone in your room or mine, but this was totally different. We weren't just hanging out between classes or when there was nothing happening on campus. You'd just been, well, violated for lack of a better word. I'd never seen you so unsure of yourself."

"Jay, I was traumatized. Nobody had ever treated me like that before. Not only did he say what he said, but he grabbed my butt when he said it. He couldn't have scared me worse if he'd jumped out of a dark alley and grabbed me."

She took a deep breath. "That's why I reacted the way I did."

I nodded. "You kissed the heck out of me."

"I did a lot more than kiss you. I practically raped you."

I shook my head hard. "You might have initiated things, but I didn't have to go along with you. I should have told you to stop; that you weren't thinking straight because of what happened. Instead, I went with the flow and hoped it would work out."

I took a deep breath and released it. "When we woke up holding each other the next day, I felt guilty for not stopping myself and hopeful that maybe our mistake could turn into a blessing."

Jenisse sighed. "And I stomped on that dream like a roach."

"Yep, that sums it up. You told me you couldn't see us as a couple, even though we'd just spent the night doing what couples in college tend to do. You said it would be too weird, and you said- - no you demanded- that we go back to being just friends. Like always, I went along with what you wanted. I didn't want to, but I felt that if I pushed too hard, you wouldn't talk to me at all."

"I wouldn't have. I was scared to face my feelings. I enjoyed spending that night with you, but I had to push you back. I wasn't ready to stop relying on one-night stands to fill my needs and reach for something more real."

I looked her in the eye. "Back then I could accept that. Shoot, a few days ago I could accept that. Now? Not so much."

I sighed. "I'm changing in ways some people might not like. I'm through with letting people use me. Wish I'd been able to get where I am now, back then."

Jenisse got so quiet I wondered if she'd fallen asleep.

"You defended me when no other man on campus would have."

She took a deep breath. "You made me feel like I was worth something, and I wasn't ready to stop feeling that way. I could have gotten sex from just about any man on campus and satisfied my physical need, but none of them could have validated me emotionally the way you did. I didn't want you to leave, and I kept you there the only way I knew how."

My God.

"Jenisse, you are worth something, but you won't be good for anyone until you know that. What happened that night jacked us both up. Twenty years is about nineteen too long to hold onto this. It's time for both of us to let it go."

I saw tears forming in her eyes.

"Jeremiah; what do we do now? We've got this out in the open; where do we go from here?"

Pride caused me to push down familiar emotions and say what had to be said.

"It's time for us to deal with reality and move on."

8

Funny how things snowball when you set out to change your life.

I figured having that talk with Jenisse would change things forever, one way or the other. For me it did. Now I knew that Jenisse only loved me like a brother and couldn't see her way clear to consider anything more. But, that's what I needed to hear. It was disappointing, but knowing was better than being on hold wondering where her heart was. Now I could see if Symone would go out with me and not wonder if I did all I could where Jenisse was concerned.

Thing is, now Jenisse was acting all weird around me. One minute she was like I'm used to and the next, she was either extra clingy or really standoffish. How am I supposed to get used to not being in love with her when she's running hot or cold?

I decided to deal with her later. Right now I had another life change to deal with. With the exception of Jenisse and Erik, my brothers and sisters owed me a combined seven thousand dollars in unpaid loans. Almost half of that debt belonged to Joel, and it was past time we talked about that.

Joel worked construction, and the job he's been on most of the fall was about to end It paid well though, just like most of his jobs. When the construction jobs were light, he worked for a couple of apartment buildings as a handyman. There's no reason in the world why Joel couldn't to pay his bills, yet he stayed in bad with creditors. Now he's earned another one. ME.

I timed it so I'd get to his house about twenty minutes after he was due in from work. Joel usually went straight home from the site so he could kick back, play with his kids and wait for Barbara to put dinner on the table. Guess it never occurred to him that she worked too and that he should cook now and then. But, that's not my business. Three thousand dollars is.

Barbara answered the door on the first ring. "Jeremiah! What brings you by?"

The sound of thundering footsteps warned me to brace for impact. This time the Twin Tornadoes couldn't budge me. After hugs and their overlapping accounts of the entirety of their school day in about ten seconds flat, Barbara shooed them back to their room so we could talk.

"Where's Joel? I thought he'd be off work by now."

Barbara peered up the stairway. Satisfied that there were no small eavesdroppers lurking at the top, she joined me on the couch and lowered her voice. "He went straight from work to get the girls' main Christmas present. A pair of bicycles."

"Upgrading from the silver scooters, huh?"

Barbara nodded. "It's time.

I took a deep breath. "You know why I'm here."

"Because Joel owes you a lot of money?"

"Nailed it. I wanted to talk to him about it face to face, but it looks like he's out spending more money."

Barbara started to say something, but I cut her off. "I know; this is for Christmas. I won't begrudge him giving his girls nice presents. Once we're past that, he and I need to have a serious conversation. I'm tired of him ducking me."

Barbara's eyes misted over. "Jeremiah, he won't listen to anybody! Not you, not Mama CC, not Mr. Thurman nobody! He's hard-headed; once he locks in, he won't change course for anybody."

She sighed. "He picks and chooses what to listen to. For example, he's listened to Mr. Thurman for years tell him how a man takes care of the family. Joel's idea of doing so means he keeps a job and that he has to pay the bills. But, he doesn't pay them on time. Sometimes he doesn't pay them at all!"

"How do you deal with that? Does stuff get turned off or discontinued?"

"No. I leave the car and the car insurance with him, but I go behind him to make sure he pays the mortgage, the water and the electric. If he doesn't do it, I do. I keep a separate account for emergencies; when he misses a bill, I pay it. And the thing is, he never notices! He thinks he can pay bills on his own schedule and nothing bad will happen."

I nodded. "I hope he doesn't still think that after the car got repoed."

"He still acts that way, even after he had to go to you to get the car back. He thinks I don't know about the repo or this latest loan you made him. I saw them when they came to get the car, and I knew the only way he could get it back that fast was to call you."

"Barbara, neither of us is doing him any favors by letting him think he's getting over."

Barbara lowered her eyes. "He won't listen to me. You don't know how many times I've tried,"

I looked her in the eye. "Try anyway. And hang in there. I'm about to give him a few object lessons in the consequences of mishandling his money. Once I'm through with him, I suspect he'll be more inclined to listen to what you have to say."

On the way home, I solidified in my mind what I'd give Joel for Christmas this year.

9

It took me a few minutes to carry all the gifts I'd received into my house.

Christmas at Mama CC's was a huge affair even if only a few of us could make it. This year, thirteen of the fifteen of us were there.

We do it up big, for the kids and for each other. 'd There were so many toys in the house that those kids could have hooked up an orphanage and still have too much to play with.

Jenisse got me a Kindle Fire HD 7 just the thing for when I have to travel. I got her that Coach bag she'd been eying for the past five months. I'd say we both did good in getting the perfect gift for one another yet again.

Of course Jenisse and I won Favorite Aunt and Uncle. They all liked their gifts from us, and thanked us without their parents having to tell them to do it.

Looks like I talked Jenisse up. My phone buzzed with a text message from her.

STILL AT MAMA CC'S. DEMONETTES RIDING BIKES LIKE IT'S THEIR JOB. IT'S DARK OUT. J & B NEED TO COME GET THEIR KIDS SO I CAN GO HOME. SERIOUSLY CONSIDERING LETTING THE AIR OUT OF THEIR TIRES.

Hilarious. She'd texted me earlier about volunteering to watch the Terrorist Twins while Joel and Barbara went to visit Barbara's mother in the hospital. Better her than me; too many of those kids want to hang out with me all the time as it is.

Suitably distracted, I put the clothes and shoes I got from the other siblings under my little tree, and the watch Mr. Thurman gave me went right on my wrist. Guess he got sick of me always pulling my phone out when I needed to know what time it was.

I tried to use this busy work to help me block thoughts of past holidays with my real family. My mom never handled any holidays all that well once Dad was gone; guess I shouldn't have been surprised when she had her stroke less than a year after he died.

Grief was a predator she just couldn't escape, and I couldn't help her fight it off. I tried to cheer her up, but it just didn't happen. She mourned herself to death and almost took me with her. Thank God for Auntie Yancey and Uncle Tovar taking me in. Not that I didn't want to be with my grandparents, but Auntie and Uncle were closer to my parents' age, and I needed that. Not that it lasted long. Thanks to diagnoses of breast and prostate cancer, I wound up with my grandparents inside of two years. And then they died too.

The phone rang and saved me from a pity party. It was Symone.

"Merry Christmas! Thank you for the gift. It was very thoughtful. And useful too."

"You're welcome. I've seen you shop. I figured a Nordstrom's gift card would come in handy."

She chuckled. "Jeremiah, you did realize the suggested limit for the Singles Pollyanna was twenty dollars."

"Like I said, I've seen you shop. Twenty bucks wouldn't even get you through the door."

"Ha ha."

We conversed for another twenty minutes before hanging up. It didn't seem that long, but it never did when the conversation was good. I didn't get around to asking her out, but the vibe was there. I'll know when it's the right time, and when it does, I'll be ready.

One of these days I'll say that and it would be true. Maybe when that day came, I'd be convinced that putting $50.00 on that Nordstrom's gift card instead of twenty wasn't me showing off for Symone.

Anyway, enough of that. I need to get ready for church tomorrow.

Just when I thought it was going to be a regular Sunday, life happened. Service was good and we were set to head over to the gym afterwards. However, I walked out of the Men's room and smack into a change of plans. Jenisse wasn't where I left her. She was about ten feet away talking to a "her type" of man. He looked like the one she drooled over at her friend's wedding, only lighter. And she was in full "he's fine and I'm gonna reel him in" mode.

I fought so hard not to roll my eyes that it gave me a headache. I don't do eavesdropping, but right about now I wished I had Superman hearing.

"Hi Jeremiah."

I turned. "Hey, Symone. How's it going?"

She chuckled. "Well, nobody in the Singles Ministry is fighting right now. I'd say it's going pretty good."

"Always a good thing. You ready to head to the gym with us?"

"That *was* the plan, but Jenisse seems a bit occupied right now."

Laughter cut into our conversation. Mr. Light Bright pantomimed a bowling motion; for some reason that set Jenisse off. They're over there laughing like folks catching up at their college homecoming.

"Give her three minutes. I've seen her in Man Mode before, and she doesn't waste a whole lot of time. He's made his case and now she's just waiting for him to ask for her number so she can close the deal."

As if on cue, he whipped his phone out and started entering digits.

"I'm guessing she either knows him from somewhere or they know someone in common. It would have taken him a few more minutes if he'd stepped to her with no credentials."

Apparently Mellow Yellow sealed the deal; he put his phone back in its holster, said something that made Jenisse giggle and strutted away like he won the Powerball.

Jenisse made her way to us.

"Sorry I kept you waiting, Jay."

I blinked and realized that Symone was gone. She vanished like the ghost of the Invisible Woman.

"Who was that guy?"

Jenisse smiled. "What do I always say was my worst time getting dumped?"

I didn't think too hard; she talked about it so much I feel like it happened to me. "That time you went out with a guy you thought was serious about you and he met someone else on your date."

"You got it. The guy I was talking to was the other "victim." Turns out Clarence's date and mine did the love at first sight thing. They got married less than a year later."

I nodded. "And your fellow dump-ee just happened to come to church today."

"Yep! And he remembered that night just like I do."

Symone rematerialized at the perfect time to redirect this conversation. "Hey, Jenisse. Ready to get your work out on?"

"I was, but I forgot to put my gym bag in the trunk today. I need to go home and get it. You guys go ahead without me, and I'll meet you there."

She was gone before either of us could say anything. Symone looked at me with a question in her eyes.

"She won't make it today. She'll go home with every intention of grabbing her gear and coming to meet us, but she'll get a call from her new friend and that will be that. She'll call one or both of us later to apologize for leaving us hanging."

Symone shook her head. "You really do know her well."

"You have no idea."

10

"You look mighty evil, Jeremiah. Who rained on your parade?"

I put the last grocery bag on Mama CC's kitchen table.

"Huh? Oh, I'm sorry. Guess my mind wandered. I have a bit of business I need to handle."

I put the food for the next family dinner where it belonged and turned to face Mama CC's hard glare. "You know Joel called."

I rolled my eyes. *Of course he came running to her thinking she would plead his case for him. Not gonna work.*

"Mama, I'm done playing with him. He's never gonna grow up and take responsibility for his actions if we all keep shielding him from consequences. Look at him now. I try to hold a grown man responsible for his debt to me and he comes crying to you."

"He said you told Barbara all his business and that you're trying to turn her against him."

"She already knew. I hope you told him that in a marriage, household finances are their business, not his or hers."

Her side eye was meaner than Mr. Thurman's.

"Joel and I are gonna have us a talk. He needs to stop trying to deflect attention off his irresponsibility and focus on paying his bills."

Mama CC heard me out and then hit me with words that almost made me return to what I committed to walk out of. "I understand, but I don't want to lose any more children."

All I could do was nod my head as she moved on to the next subject. She motioned me to sit down.

"Time for a Mama talk, okay?"

Oh Lord, this won't be good.

"Jenisse called, too."

"Son, I've had my eye on you and Jenisse since the day she became part of our lives. When you came to me talking about this Jenisse girl you'd met, I had to get to know her. And when I did, I realized she needed me every bit as much as you did. I also saw from Day One that you were in love with her. Unless I miss my guess, you still are."

I couldn't open my mouth to tell her she was wrong, so I took the diplomatic route. "We've talked it out and we've decided to be the brother and sister we already are. I'm moving on."

Her eyes widened. "Is that so?"

"Yes ma'am."

"You have your eye on someone?"

I couldn't grin wide enough. "Yeah."

"Go slow, Jeremiah. You moving on is good, but if you're not fully purged from your feelings for Jenisse, don't waste someone else's time while you're trying to prove that you are."

Having said her piece, Mama CC got up and started putting the food away.

"Time for me to go, Mama. I've got my business trip to Dallas coming up, and I still haven't packed."

She rolled her eyes. "Yes, well, you'd best get to it. Your bags won't pack themselves."

I drove home on automatic pilot. It'll be good to get away for a while, especially since my whole family seemed determined to act up all at once. I needed to call Joel before I left, and see if I could lay the groundwork for us finding some common ground.

I barely got in the door and got out my suitcase before someone rang my doorbell. I opened it and found Erik on the other side. He stepped past me and into my house like he paid my mortgage.

"Hey, you wanna come in?"

Erik got comfortable in my favorite chair. "Why are you here when you could be out on a date?"

"I could ask you the same thing, but you found somebody. Talia must be awesome. Why aren't you with her, now? Better yet, why haven't you told your parents yet? Oh yeah, I forgot, you're not talking to them."

"Man, quit trying to deflect. I know why you're not trying to get out there. It's Jenisse. You the only dude I know who's whipped by someone he's not even in a relationship with!"

I looked up from my packing and gave Erik my best laser-beam side-eye, which he skillfully ignored. I bent over and grabbed a shirt I dropped and aimed my butt in his general direction.

"I don't remember actually inviting you over here, you know. I'm trying to pack."

He ignored me completely. "You been doing this since college. How long you gonna keep this up? Forget Twelve Years A Slave- I'ma start calling you Twenty Years A Brother."

"Give it a rest."

Erik flicked his wrist. 'Whipped."

"All right Secret Squirrel, don't make me hurt you. Better yet, don't make me tell your mama who you're dating."

That shut him down long enough for me to tell him that I broke off a relationship I was never really in.

"That's good. You're not Adam. There's more than one woman you can choose from."

"The same applies to you. Seems to me if you're dating someone and you can't tell your family about her, maybe you don't need to be dating her. You kinda old for teenage rebellion. About ten years too old, to be exact."

"Whatever. I'm on my way to meet Talia now."

He left without making any further wisecracks. That told me I nailed him. Shoot, he knew he was wrong for choosing a woman over his parents. I bet she doesn't even know why he hadn't introduced her to them after seeing him for almost a year.

I returned to packing; at the same time, I wondered how much longer Erik would keep not talking to his folks. Something he said stuck in my head. I'm not Adam and Jenisse wasn't Eve. I needed to broaden my horizons.

I placed the call before I chickened out. Symone answered faster than I thought.

"Hi Jeremiah!"

"Hey, how's it going?"

"Can't complain. Wish I was going away like you though. I could use a break from the daily routine."

"Trust me, this won't be much of a break. I'm going for work."

"How long will you be in Dallas?"

"Four days. The conference I'm going to is two and half days, but I'm going a little early to catch up with one of my boys from college."

Symone giggled again. "Uh oh, the dreaded college friend. Have fun, but try not to get arrested before your conference starts."

"Not likely, unless they're rounding up guys to send to the Geek Relocation center."

I did an above average nerdish snort-laugh, which made Symone laugh so hard it sounded like she almost dropped her phone.

I heard her struggle to catch her breath. "You mean you weren't the men my mother always warned me about?"

"Trust me, we were not those men. We were the ones those men elbowed aside to get to the women."

Her laughter sounded like sweet music. "Maybe you should have passed on the plaid high-water pants."

My laugh got out before I could check it. "Dang Symone, did you see college pictures or something? And I thought the Urkel look was gonna get me somewhere."

We bantered back and forth for a few minutes until I felt comfortable enough to get to the real point of this call.

"Say, I was wondering, would you like to go out when I get back from Nerdland? I'll need some real company by then."

Silence. That's never good.

"Um, yeah! Yes, that would be nice."

A huge weight lifted off my shoulders. "Good. Well, um, I'll call you when I get back and we can set it up."

"Works for me."

11

At first I couldn't figure out why I was so excited at coming home from a trip I'd looked forward to for so long. It hit me as the flight attendant announced our descent into the Philadelphia airport—it was Symone. She agreed to go out with me!

The soft bump of the plane landing jolted me out of my thoughts. When it stopped rolling, I retrieved my carry-on bag from the overhead compartment, did the same for the short lady sitting next to me and joined the herd of bodies flowing off the plane. I hoped Joel was waiting for me. All I wanted to do was get my suitcase, get in his/my car and get home.

I took my phone off Airplane mode, and to my complete lack of surprise, it pinged with about fifteen new messages. All of them were sent during the flight, and most of them were from someone begging.

WLCUM BACK. HIT ME UP WHEN U LAND- ND 2 ASK U SMTHNG
HOPE U HAD A GOOD FLIGHT. CAN U STILL WATCH THE KIDS NEXT WEEKEND?
HOPE U HAD FUN IN DALLAS. CALL ME SO WE CAN TALK ABOUT THAT LOAN
CALL ME WHEN YOU GET SETTLED IN. NEED TO ASK U SOMETHING
WELCOME BACK! SCHL PLAY 2MORROW- CAN U COME?
HOPE U HAD A GOOD TIME. I'LL B THERE WHEN YOUR FLIGHT LANDS.
HIT ME UP WHEN U LAND- LOTS 2 TALK ABOUT

That last one was from Erik. Translation: "I need you to tell my parents something exciting that I'm doing because I'm still not speaking to them."

I'll deal with him once I get my bags and get back home.

I swear I'm gonna beat every square inch of Joel's behind when I catch him.

Before I left, I tapped him for my ride home. I just saw his text from two hours ago telling me he would be here. There was no reason why I should still be here waiting, and none I could figure out that would keep him from answering his phone

Nobody else answered their phones either. Deborah. Straight to voicemail. Ruth. Same. Jenisse. No answer, full voicemail box. Joel again. Nope. And again. Still no answer. Erik. Probably out with Talia and has his phone on silent.

Why am I still sitting here an hour later? *Somebody* needs to answer their phone.

Okay, somebody who actually feels comfortable driving at night. Guess I won't be calling Mr. Thurman or Mama CC.

I resisted the urge to throw my Kindle Fire across the Baggage Claim area.

Joel couldn't be bothered to come get me? That punk wouldn't even have a car if I hadn't paid to get it back from repo.

Forget him. I'm getting outta here. I have the Uber app on my phone. Time to use it.

My Uber driver was a smiling Jamaican woman. She tried to make pleasant conversation, but I was too busy plotting revenge against Joel to engage. She gave up after a few attempts, and let me ride the rest of the way home in silence.

I walked in my front door, threw my suitcase down in disgust and headed straight for the shower. I had no idea why traveling felt like such hard work when all I did was sit. I sat on the plane for a couple hours, sat in the baggage claim waiting for Joel and then sat in the back of the Uber car.

The shower calmed me down some, but not nearly enough. I scrounged for sweatpants and cursed Joel to the third and fourth generation at the same time. My phone rang and interrupted my thoughts on how dead I was gonna make Joel for leaving me hanging. My jaw dropped when I saw who was calling me.

"Hey, Symone!"

"Hello yourself, Weary Traveler. Are you home yet or still at the airport?"

"I just got in not long ago."

I told her how Joel left me hanging. "You should have called me. I would have come to get you."

I grinned so hard I'm sure she could see it over the phone. "I appreciate it, but that never should have been a thought. I have too much family in this state to be left at the airport. Thank God for Uber. I might have had to live there like Tom Hanks in that movie."

Symone laughed. "I'm sure you weren't there that long, but I get your point."

A thought popped into my head. Before we broke up from what never was, I assumed I was going to take Jenisse to the next social event on her calendar. I allowed 'assume' to fly out the window, and embraced a better idea.

"Symone, would you like to come to the Urban League dance with me on Saturday?"

"I'd love to!"

"Great!"

We went over the details for the dance.

"Well Jay, I guess I'll hang up now. You probably have jet lag knocking on your door just waiting to get at you."

"Yeah, I'm starting to feel it."

We said our good nights and hung up.

When I got in the house, all I wanted to do was shower and sleep, but not now. I've been to a million of these formal dances with Jenisse, but all of a sudden, it felt like I was about to go somewhere brand new.

"Jay, I'm sorry, man. I completely lost track of time last night."

I was too pissed off to open my mouth right this second. I needed to count to ten and then say something, or else I might breathe fire on Joel. Mondays already had a bad reputation. I decided to not add murdering my little brother to that rep.

"Did you or did you not text me somewhere around five o'clock telling me you would be there to meet my flight?"

Joel wouldn't look me in the eye or even get too close. I guess he thought I'd punch him out in his own house. Trust me, I was tempted.

"Yeah."

"So, what happened between then and two and a half hours later that kept you from coming to get me?"

"I was helping my boy Tarron move. He helped me when me and Barbara moved in our house, and I had to return the favor."

"Either you lost track of time or you were trapped under something heavy. Which was it?"

He started to answer, but I cut him off. "Wait, there's a third option. You're trifling."

He whipped his head around and glared at me. I was so not impressed.

"I'm glad you're capable of thinking of someone besides yourself, but you couldn't do both? You couldn't help Tarron until, say, 7:00 and then tell him you had to go pick your brother up from the airport at 7:30?"

Joel opened his mouth, closed it and stopped trying to defend himself.

"You agreed to pick me up! How you gonna do that and forget all about me? I suppose you and your boy got to playing X-Box and that was that."

He at least had the decency to look embarrassed. I must have nailed it.

"Boy, you better listen to me good, because I'm only gonna say this once. I am through with you treating me like crap until you need something. If you need to borrow money, I'm your best friend. Time to do something for me or pay back what you borrowed? You're ghost.''"

I forced myself to slow my breathing down. If I got any angrier, I was either gonna punch Joel in the face or bust a blood vessel in my forehead.

"J, man, I'm sorry. You right. After we got all his stuff in, T started talking junk about whooping me in Madden. I showed him how wrong he was, but I forgot what time it was until it was way too late."

"Apology accepted. Next time though, call me. I was wondering if you got in an accident or something."

"How'd you get home?"

Oh, now you care. "Thanks to you and the rest of my trifling family—Uber."

I got up to leave, and then turned back to Joel. "I need you to grow up."

I reached for the door knob and stopped. "You told me three paychecks ago you were gonna start paying me back for un repo-ing your car. When's that gonna happen for real?"

He shrugged. "I just paid all the bills. I'll get you on the next paycheck."

"No you didn't pay *all* the bills or we wouldn't be having this discussion, Joel. Get it together. For yourself, for your wife and for your kids. This immature crap's getting old, Little Brother. I'm not playing with you anymore, and neither will anyone else"

I walked out of his house without saying another word.

12

My phone pinged for about the 386th time in the past two hours since I got home. I glanced at the number, saw it was yet another sibling asking for stuff and let it go to voicemail.

Mmm hmm. I couldn't reach nary a one of them when I was stuck at the airport, but now that one of them is having a crisis, look out.

One of the hundreds of calls had to be from Joel. Operation Teach Joel A Life Lesson was an unqualified success. It was well worth taking a day off.

Part I of The Lesson. Don't be predictable. I knew where Joel parked his car. Contrary to his belief, it wasn't as safe as he and his coworkers thought. I caught the bus to get up DuPont Highway; got off right across the street from where Joel parked. I made sure nobody was looking, used my spare key and made off with the car, which, thanks to the contract he signed with me, was now mine. Once I took the car to the garage-sized storage area I rented and secured it, I caught another bus home.

Part II. When you don't pay your bills for long enough and fail to make an acceptable payment arrangement with your most determined creditor, you may find that your creditors have attached your wages. The process wasn't as tough as one might think. Now Joel will pay me the agreed upon $150.00 per month whether he wants to or not.

More overlapping pings. Messages came in so hard and fast it sounded like someone using sonar. Might as well see what the family's so up in arms about.

J, HIT ME BACK. SOMEBODY STOLE MY CAR!

JAY, JOEL'S CAR WAS STOLEN FROM HIS JOB SITE! L CALL HIM- HE'S FREAKING OUT (BARBARA)

J, JOEL NEEDS TO KNOW HOW TO FILE A POLICE REPORT ON A STOLEN CAR. YOURS GOT STOLEN A FEW YEARS BACK- CAN YOU HELP THE BROTHER OUT? (ERIK)

J, MAN, WHERE YOU AT? I NEED SOME BROTHERLY ADVICE! (JOEL)

Time to yank his chain a little with a quick text.

DID YOU CALL THE INSURANCE COMPANY YET?

His return text confirmed what I already knew.

DON'T HAVE INSURANCE YET

Figures. Half of the three grand Joel owed me was the fine he got for driving uninsured last year. I recall threatening to run him over with his own car if he didn't get insured quick, fast and in a hurry. He's been driving uninsured all this time.

THIS IS WHY I TOLD YOU TO GET SOME. NOW YOU CAN'T FILE A CLAIM TO REPLACE IT. WHAT DO YOU PLAN TO DO TO GET AROUND?

No answer. He was probably too busy being pissed off at the fact that I was right to think that far ahead.

The pings changed up some. I looked and saw group messages instead of the individual texts I had been getting. With me not responding, they had to create a plan of action. Jenisse stepped in to pick up the Demonettes from daycare. Deborah volunteered to pick Barbara up from work.

My smile spread across my face. It was nice to know they knew how to get things done without me doing them.

My phone rang. Erik. Perfect timing. He was uniquely qualified to help with the next phase of the plan. "What up man?"

"Jay, where've you been? Joel's car was stolen, he's freaking out and Oldest Brother is nowhere to be found. Where you been?"

"I just texted him. He's definitely freaking out, not only because the car was stolen, but also because he doesn't have insurance."

"What? After all that mess last year he's still driving uninsured? Moron."

I had to laugh. "Can't argue with that."

"Jay, why weren't you surprised to hear that Joel's car was stolen?"

"Because I stole it."

I told him how Jeremiah McAllister Repo Services operated. By the time I finished the story, Erik was gasping for breath from laughing.

"Aw man, that's classic! Didn't think you had that in you."

"Neither did Joel. That's why it worked. Now I need you to help me out if you're willing."

I outlined his proposed part in the plan, and he finally stopped laughing long enough to agree.

"I'll get on it first thing tomorrow. Just let me know when you want me to go ahead."

This time yesterday, the 8,400,379 messages from my family all asked for my help. Today the tone was different, but the volume of messages was the same. My phone buzzed so many times that it almost burned a hole in my pocket.

I didn't know whether to laugh or laugh harder as I read through some of them.

I CANT BLV U ATTACHED JOELS WAGES. THAT'S COLD. (Ruth)

DID U RLLY GARNISH JOELS CHECK RGHT AFTR HS CR WS STLN? (Deborah)

JOEL JST CLLED ME UP CUSSING. DID U ATTACH HIS PYCHK? (Jenisse)

Three messages were from Joel. Each one called me out my name and told me how cold-hearted I was for having his wages attached right after his car was stolen.

A message from Symone invited me to the Singles Ministry meeting tonight. That one I planned to accept.

I left work, connected my Bluetooth, and listened to the remainder of the messages as I drove home.

I was barely inside my house before someone pounded on my door like it was a police raid.

I opened the door and found just who I expected. "Are you out of your #@%$ mind?!? What the #^@$?! is wrong with you?"

Joel stormed into my house like he lived here.

"Hello to you too, Joel. Something wrong?"

Joel got so far in my face I could taste the ham sandwich he ate for lunch." "You know what's wrong, $%*&#! You attached my #@!#! Check! You took my car, didn't you? Why you put me through all that crap about insurance and police reports when you had the car all this time?"

I stepped back to a safe distance before I hurt him. "First of all, stop cussing at me before I punch you in your throat. Second, you need a Tic Tac real bad. Third, congratulations on being smart enough to figure out what happened. I didn't think you were. Needless to say, I did what I had to do."

The look on his face was priceless.

"Why the...why you had to take my car?"

"I didn't take your car. I took my car."

I paused for effect. His nostrils flared so wide I could have inserted three fingers up each with ease.

"Let me break this down to you. When I agreed to pay for you to get your car back from repo, we signed an agreement. When you didn't keep your word, I had to keep the word I made to myself to take care of my business."

His silence spoke volumes.

I went to the kitchen and got a bottle of water. I drank half before I returned and let him have the rest of my spiel. "Once I have the three back payments and you can provide proof of insurance, we'll talk about me returning the car. Until then, 'Precious' stays with me."

"Where's it at?"

"At the Jeremiah McAllister Repo Yard."

Silence.

"Can I at least get my stuff out?"

"Your stuff is in the Repo Yard's storage. There's a one-time $35.00 fee to get it out. Cash only. Anything still in the car after thirty days gets thrown out."

Joel cussed me so hard I wondered if he had undiagnosed Tourette's.

"Much money as you owe me, I'm the one who should be cussing. This was just the latest time you came to me for money without even *thinking* about paying me back from the other times. Since you clearly forgot, you still owe me bail money and that fine you got slapped with for driving uninsured."

Dead silence. If I hadn't heard him breathing, I would have sworn that he had died on his feet.

"Those are my terms. Deal with it."

Joel mumbled something profane under his breath.

"One more thing. McAllister Repo has excellent security. Should anyone manage to locate the storage area and try to breach said security to liberate any repossessed vehicle on our premises, they would find that said vehicle has been re-keyed and fitted with a different alarm system. And yes, we do prosecute car thieves."

I stopped Joel's next round of cussing with a warning. "Whatever you were gonna say about me, save it. I don't know when you're gonna grow up and stop always trying to use people, but it won't happen with me ever again. And don't waste your time complaining to Mama CC about this; I told her and Mr. Thurman what I had in mind before I did it. Bad enough you called everyone else in the family to tell them what a jerk I am. Whiner."

"How you gonna leave my wife and kids with no car, man? You ain't no kinda brother to me, acting like that."

I moved back into bad breath and throat-punching range. "I'm the best brother you can have. Why? Because I'm taking your trifling butt out of Pampers and putting you on the potty. It's about five years past time for you to man up. And I don't want to hear about Barbara and the girls. You weren't thinking about them when you jacked up your family's money and left them in the lurch. Don't even try to put this on me. I've been there for you when no one else was. And since I still am, let's talk about you being 'no kind' of a father. You don't get it together and tame them two girls, you and Barbara are gonna have more heartache than you ever thought possible."

An extremely pissed off Joel stormed out of my house. Just as well. I had nothing more to say to him, and if he'd stayed to argue much longer, I would have been late for the Singles Ministry meeting.

Half an hour later, I was in my car headed to the church. And of course the second my behind hit the seat, my phone rang again. I turned on my Bluetooth so I could take the call and get on the road at the same time.

"Jay, thank God you picked up. I'm stranded. My car just broke down."

Time for another life lesson. Didn't think I'd have to do this again so soon.

"Jenisse, why are you calling me?

"Because my engine practically exploded and I need help."

"Sorry, I didn't make myself clear. I meant to say that last time I checked, women usually call their boyfriends when they have issues like this. You lose Clarence's number?"

"He couldn't get away from work."

"And?"

"I told you, he's working. I'm not going to be one of those needy high-maintenance women who demands her man leave his job because I broke a nail."

"But it's okay for you to ask me to drop what I'm doing right now to rescue you?"

Jenisse raised her voice. "That's different."

"How?"

"You're my brother, you're supposed to be there for me. Clarence is someone I'm seeing."

"Are you in a safe location?"

"Yeah. I'm at Applebee's, in the parking lot."

"Good. Ought to make it easy for AAA to find you."

"WHAT?"

"Jenisse, I'm not coming. I'm on my way to meet someone. You have a AAA membership. Now would be a good time to put it to use."

I hung up before she could protest any further.

13

My phone wouldn't stop pinging. Message after message, same old same old. Gotta love family drama.

J, WHAT U DID 2 JOEL IS WRNG!

J, ABOUT TIME U DID TOUGH LUV ON JOEL

J, CHK YR EMAIL. JUST SNT U $$$ BY PAYPAL. I DON'T WANT U 2 ATTCH MY CHK NXT LOL

CAN U WTCH MY KIDS 2NIGHT?

After about the 59th ping, I heard a feminine chuckle from my passenger seat. "You're sure popular tonight."

I hoped that my response was as nonchalant as I needed it to be. "More business as usual, Symone. My brothers and sisters are blowing me up to either tear me a new one over what I did to Joel or to ask why it took me so long to get after him."

Another message pinged in. I readjusted my phone in the cup holder where I set it and indicated to Symone to look at the screen so she could see what I'm hearing. She took one look and cracked up.

YOUR BEING TWO MEAN TOO JOEL

"Autocorrect must be killing this text."

I smiled. "No, she just can't spell. And she hates when I do this."

I dictated a reply that cracked Symone up some more.

I GUESS YOU MEANT TO SAY "**YOU'RE** BEING **TOO** MEAN **TO** JOEL." IF YOU'RE GONNA TAKE HIS SIDE FROM ALL THE WAY ACROSS THE COUNTRY, AT LEAST GET IT RIGHT.

Symone sagged against the door laughing. "That's COLD!"

I shrugged. "She lives in Wyoming. What's she gonna do, come after me?"

We laughed and talked until we arrived at the hotel. I couldn't believe how self-conscious I felt It was as if this was my first ever date.

I made sure to get out of the car first and open her door before she did it herself. She appreciated the effort and told me so.

"Jeremiah, this is great! Thank you so much for inviting me. I love the Sheraton's ballroom."

We walked through the lobby to the ballroom. At the door I handed over our tickets, took her arm and escorted her to our assigned table. This night would be a bit tricky for me. The Symone's blue gown spoke to me. It hugged her in the right places and the neckline, although not revealing, made my eyes want to linger where they shouldn't. If I'm not careful I might get caught.

"Jay! I wasn't sure you were coming. Have a seat."

I almost laughed out loud as I heard the unspoken "without Jenisse" in Mama CC's statement.

"Aren't you the one who always tells me I need to get out more? Well, here I am."

I remembered my manners. "Oh, this is…"

Mama CC cut me off and hugged Symone before I could introduce her.

"It's good to see you again, young lady."

Symone giggled. "It seems strange to see you outside of Women's Fellowship, Mrs. CC."

"Lord knows we need not spend all our time in church. We'd be half crazy inside of a week!"

We all laughed. Symone looked at her watch. "When did Jenisse say she'd get here?"

On cue, Hurricane Jenisse blew into the hotel ballroom, alone. She found her assigned table, sat down and scanned the room. Symone raised a hand to get her attention and waved her over.

Her nostrils flared and she looked like she was about to shoot lasers out of her eyes like that guy from the X-Men. I've been on the other end of that look before. Clarence was surely standing in the need of prayer right about now.

Symone put a comforting hand on Jenisse's bare arm. "What's wrong?"

Jenisse took what I assumed was supposed to be a calming breath. It didn't help

"Clarence waited *until twenty minutes ago* to call and let me know he wouldn't be able to escort me here tonight. It seems his team is working, and as a good boss, he wouldn't ask them to give up their entire weekend unless he was willing to do the same."

Mama CC shook her head in disbelief. "I understand having to work late, but didn't he know this was coming before tonight?"

Jenisse threw her hands up. "I'm not thinking about him tonight. I thought about staying home, but then both tickets would've gone to waste."

Awkward didn't even scratch the surface of this mess. It turned out that one couple at our table wouldn't be here, which meant that Jenisse could permanently defect from hers. Oh joy. I go for a first date and wind up on a reality show.

Screw this. Jenisse's situation with Clarence was none of my business. My business was to focus on Symone.

About three minutes into a good conversation with Symone, that plan was shot to sunshine. "Jay, can you get me a drink?"

Crap. Should have known Jenisse would figure out a way to be a pain. Clarence wasn't here, so she thought I'd fill in to do date things. Problem was, I had a date. I bet this was her scheme to pay me back for not coming to get her when her car died the other day.

Mama CC sized up the situation and stepped in. She nudged Mr. Thurman, who sprang into action.

"Jenisse, I'm about to go get CC something. I can get yours while I'm up. What're you in the market for?"

I asked Symone if she wanted a drink. She contributed to the 'save Jeremiah's butt' fund by asking me to get her a Sprite. I was relieved; 'because I needed to get away from the table like yesterday.

I clapped Mr. Thurman on the back as we approached the bar. "Thanks for the save. That was about to get ugly."

Mr. Thurman chuckled. "Son, I've seen worse than that in my day, but let me give you some advice. Symone is your date and your priority. You talk to Symone. You dance with Symone. You treat Symone like she's the only one at that table. We'll handle your sister. You got me?"

I nodded and gave Mr. Thurman another clap on the back.

When we returned to the table, I followed Mr. Thurman's lead. We doted on Symone and Mama CC like queens.

"Symone, how's the Singles Ministry treating you these days? I hope your members aren't giving you too hard a time."

She laughed. "Not any harder than usual, Mr. Thurman. We still get our share of folks who join up expecting it to be Christian Mingle or Plenty Of Fish. We keep telling them that we're there to learn to be content as singles, not to help them find a man or a woman. Unfortunately, most of them tune me out when I get to the part about being content whether being single is a short visit or a lifetime stay.

I nodded. "Having been to the last meeting, I can confirm quite a few who think it's the Church Dating Ministry. You executive committee folks have got your work cut out for you."

Just then, the band introduced themselves and started playing their first song. At the first notes of "To Be Real," Mama CC began to snap her fingers while she moved to the beat. "Aw sookie sookie now!"

She grabbed Mr. Thurman's hand and hustled him out to the dance floor. The look on Symone's face told me everything I needed to know. I took her hand and we followed Mama CC and Mr. Thurman. We found a good spot and started dancing. I was getting into it when something made me look over to our table.

Jenisse sat there looking like the Grinch Who Stole Christmas.

I usually get a lot done on Mondays, but not this one. I couldn't get Saturday out of my mind. That was the best time I'd had in years. There's something about Symone, something I hadn't seen until we spent time together like that.

A phone call from a client broke me out of pleasant memories, but something hit me as soon as I hung up. I knew what it is about Symone. She wasn't Jenisse. That alone helped me to see how much of a good thing that really was.

My cell phone rang. When I didn't answer, a text immediately followed. A second text overlapped the first.

CAN YOU WATCH MY KIDS FRIDAY NIGHT?

CAN YOU WATCH MY KIDS SATURDAY NIGHT?

My reply to both texts: NO!

I didn't have plans yet, but I intended to ask Symone out again for this weekend when I call her tonight.

Despite Jenisse trying to cast a thundercloud over the whole evening, we had a great time at the dance. Symone didn't play those kinds of games with me. There was a huge difference between how Jenisse treated me and how Symone did. I'm glad she gave me the chance to explore that difference.

Three more begging texts pinged my phone, each from a sibling who like Joel, owed me money. Since the Joel garnishment, I've had a few discrete conversations with some of them asking when they might start their repayment plan. They each had a sudden onset of Joel-itis, which meant that they conveniently forgot how much they owed. Since I kept great records, I had an accurate account for each.

I answered each 'begging text' with SEE ME SUNDAY AT DINNER. As soon as I hit send, I received another text.

This one was from Erik letting me know we could get together today after work to put the finishing touches on our plan. Once we do that, this Sunday's family dinner would become legendary.

14

"**O**kay, the kids are in the den watching Frozen for about the 600th time. While we're all here, I need to get some stuff said. Listen carefully, 'cause I'm only gonna say this once."

Mama CC's eyebrows went up higher than I thought possible. Mr. Thurman had a satisfied expression on his face, as if he read my mind and knew what was coming.

I took a deep breath. "Except for Jenisse, I've loaned money to everybody in this room at some point. Erik is the only one who ever paid me back. As of today, thinking that you'll never repay me, ends." I pointed my finger at each person indebted to me. "You have thirty days to either pay it back in full or get with me to make arrangements.

Their stunned expressions had no effect on what else I had to say.

"Baby sitting. I will no longer take the entire tribe of Benjamin by myself. I need a minimum of three days' notice, and I need you to send snacks along with your kids. No snacks, no entry. I'm serious about needing notice. Ask me the day of and you better be having emergency surgery."

I stared Joel down. "Going forward, anyone who drops their kids off without first clearing it with me will die a slow and painful death."

The others stopped short of laughing out loud. Everyone in the family knew what I did after Joel, child-bombed me with his non-public-ready daughters.

I made eye contact with everyone while I paced around the room. "Last thing. I am sick and tired of this being a one-way street. I don't ask for help often, but when I do, I would appreciate it if folks would at least answer the phone and tell me if they can or can't help me out.

I strolled back to the coffee table and picked up my phone. "I'm done. Think that over, and decide when you want to chat me up about your loan statuses. I know you all know my cell number. But do me a favor though, and call me tomorrow. Tonight, I have a date."

The stunned looks on everybody's faces were priceless. Jenisse's most of all.

I thought I heard Mr. Thurman chuckle, but I didn't stick around to confirm; I put my phone in my pocket, pulled out my car keys and walked toward the door like a boss.

For some reason Joel thought he could shame me into what he wanted with a public display of his ignorance. He caught up to me in the foyer and tried to read me the riot act in a tone seasoned with chastisement.

"J, I don't know what's going on with you lately, but it needs to stop. You got to get off your high horse and act like our brother again."

My mind went blank at the sheer stupidity coming out of his mouth. He took that as a sign to keep demonstrating his ignorance. "Look man, because of whatever's going on with you, my wife and kids are suffering. Barbara has to leave the house two hours earlier so she can get the girls to daycare and then herself to work on time."

"Yeah, I heard she's suffering, but not because of me. You're her husband. It's up to you, not me to take care of your family." I leaned in close. "Personally, if I were her I would have kicked you out the first day you let me struggle on the bus with them kids while you carpooled to work."

Joel walked away. Since he just gave me the perfect opening, I figured now was the time to completely ruin his day. I pulled out my phone and called Erik. I used my outdoor voice.

"Smurf? I'm at the family dinner. Yeah, I laid down the law. Yeah, everybody's still here. I need you to make that move."

"I'm on it. Give me five minutes."

Heads snapped around and Joel came a runnin'. He got right in my face and gave me the stink eye. "You're still here? I thought you had a date. Or somebody else to demand money from."

I narrowed my eyes in my best "You idiot" stare. "Joel, I was going to do this on the low, but since you want to try to call me out, we're doing this right here, right now. Barbara, can you come over here please?"

Barbara's expression made it clear that she had no idea what was going on.

I returned to my outdoor voice. "You've been enduring serious transportation issues. Unlike Joel, who we all know is at fault for this, I really do have a heart. I asked Erik if he could help me alleviate said issues, and out of the kindness of his heart, he agreed."

My phone rang on cue. Erik was on the line.

"I'm here."

"Okay. I got you on speaker. Talk to Barbara."

Erik's voice echoed through the phone. "Hey, sis what's up? Heard you got a bit of a car trouble. Sorry 'bout that, but I have a cure for what ails you. I got a new ride last month. I haven't gotten rid of the other one yet. Wanna see it."

I opened the front door so we could all see Erik behind the wheel of his bright blue 2004 Dodge Neon, now parked directly behind my car.

We all made our way to the sidewalk. As I expected, Erik stayed behind the wheel instead of getting out of the car. He talked to Barbara through the open passenger side window. "I'm sure you all remember the Bloopty? (Blue Hoopty) Or as y'all like to call it, the Smurf-mobile."

Everybody chuckled. Erik hated that name, and was glad to retire the car so he could put up with one less short joke at his expense.

"I took it for an oil change and a battery charge a few days ago. It's old, but it runs and will get somebody from point A to point B until a better option pops up. Barbara, if you wanna be that somebody, I'm cool with it."

He tossed me the key, which I handed to Barbara. She blinked back a tear and went around the car to hug him hard. Joel's eyes lit up, and he followed her. That was my cue.

"Joel, don't get too excited. Erik put Barbara on his insurance, not you. She is the only one not named Erik who can legally drive it."

As the rest of the family watched, Erik stepped out of the car and got in Joel's face. "I'm glad you chose to try and call Jay out, because I want the whole family to hear me say this to you. This car is still *in my* name. I am allowing Barbara to borrow it for as long as she needs because she and the girls need reliable transportation. You have demonstrated that you know how to get where you need to go, so keep on doing whatever it is you're doing. If she wants to drive you someplace in my car, that's her business. I left the title in the glove compartment and I attached a note in case she ever gets pulled over so the police would know she has my permission to drive my car. But if I catch *you* driving it, your butt belongs to me. Matter of fact, if you even dream about driving my car, you better wake up and call me to apologize. You think Jay did you dirty? I catch your butt driving my car and I'm calling the cops to report it stolen and you for driving uninsured."

I didn't think someone as dark-skinned as Joel could turn that red. The vein popping out on his forehead told me he still had bad memories of the $1500.00 fine he got for driving uninsured last time.

"And should that happen, you would want to just stay in jail. You can go for a drive in that car if you want to, but I guarantee you that if you do, I'll come over your house and walk you like a dog."

I heard snickers in the background, but Erik wasn't amused.

I swear I saw steam coming out of Joel's ears. He was hotter than Dallas in August. He looked like he was about to turn into the Hulk any second now. I took over from Erik and stared him down. "You got anything else to say about how bad I'm treating you and your wife and kids?"

Joel was quieter than a mime in the library.

"I thought not. Come on, Smurf. I'll drop you off home."

"Hello Erik."

Erik took a deep breath and released it. "Hey, Mom. Dad. How's it going?"

Mr. Thurman locked eyes with his son. "Could be better."

I slipped behind the wheel of my car. Erik nodded to his folks, spun on his heel and got in beside me.

15

I stood and stretched, painfully aware that I'd spent the last hour and a half of a two-hour movie with my right arm draped around the adjoining seat. I shook the bloodless limb in an attempt to revive it.

"Are you all right?"

Symone's soft inquiry helped massage the pins and needles out of my arm.

"I'm fine. Besides, it was for a good cause. This arm didn't give its life in vain. I'll take a numb arm for good company any time."

She laughed and handed me the remains of our cinematic snack. I tossed the popcorn and Raisinet boxes into the nearest trashcan as we headed for the exit.

We talked about the movie and rehashed our favorite scenes as we drove. We were still laughing when Jake's Wayback Burgers came into view.

"Jeremiah, can we stop?"

I pulled over and found a parking space. "I can't believe you're hungry after all the junk we ate."

"Not so much hungry as craving some ice cream. They make milkshakes here so thick they're like sundaes."

"Sounds good to me."

After we placed our orders, I reached for my wallet. Symone stopped me by putting her hand on top of mine.

"You paid for everything tonight. The least I can do is treat you here."

It went against my grain, but I let her pay. We took our shakes to one of the tables instead of taking them to go.

"Jeremiah, thanks again for tonight. I've had a really great time."

"Me too. I have to admit; I was kind of nervous about even asking you."

Symone smiled. "Let me guess. The ball was one thing, because Jenisse was there and it wasn't a real date. This is completely different."

"Can't fool you, can I?"

I sampled a bit of my orange shake to buy a few seconds. "This does feel different to me, and I like it. I didn't think I'd feel this way, but I really enjoyed tonight. It's great being here with you, just the two of us."

The warmth that radiated from Symone's pleasant expression gave me the courage to continue. "I, uh, I'd really like to keep seeing you. You know, to find out if there's anything for us outside of just being friends."

Symone savored the taste of vanilla and banana before answering. I held my breath and waited for her to answer.

"Jeremiah, I can honestly say that I had a great time tonight. I'm really enjoying myself; in fact, I'll hate to see tonight come to an end. But when it does, I'm not sure it's a good idea if you and I continue to spend time together like this."

I closed my eyes and took a spoonful of orange sherbet. It tasted like disappointment.

"Will you tell me why?"

Symone closed her eyes, as if firing off a quick prayer.

"You already know why, Jeremiah. You're out with me now, but you're not totally over Jenisse."

I could only imagine the look on my face. "Maybe you didn't get the memo, but I'm done with all that. We'll always be family connected, but I'm not letting her play with my heart any more. Jenisse and I are brother and sister. No more, no less."

"If I believed that were true, I wouldn't be out with you right now. I would've given you more time to get over her before accepting a date with you, and I would have told you as much when you asked."

"Then why did you come?"

"Because I needed to talk to you. God gave me permission to accept when you asked me out, and I'm glad about that. Until the ball and this, I haven't been out in a while, and I do enjoy your company. But, if you and I were to start dating now, it wouldn't go anywhere. You have some things you still need to deal with."

She paused, as if seeking guidance as to what to say next.

"Whether you believe it or not, you're a good man with a lot to offer. Any woman in her right mind, and yes that includes me, should want to spend this kind of time with you, but you don't need to be with just any woman. You deserve God's best."

I chuckled. "If that's the case, why don't you want to date me?"

Symone laughed. "Never let it be said you're not smooth. My point is that you and Jenisse have major unresolved issues. Everybody who knows you both can see you have feelings for each other. It's so obvious my thickheaded brother figured it out. He wanted to ask Jenisse for a date, but one look at you and her in church told him not to bother. When you two are together, your body language screams "It's complicated.""

I finished the remainder of my shake and pushed the cup aside. "Great. I finally get to where I can let Jenisse go and you're pushing me back at her."

"It's not so much me pushing you back at her as it is me not wanting to inherit any of her issues. One of those is that you haven't fully let go."

Symone took a deep breath. "I don't know all the details, and I don't want to. But, it's clear that you haven't had enough time to be single. Until you talk things out with her and get some closure, you aren't free to date me or anyone else because part of you is still with her."

I felt my eyes get wide, and I had to make an effort not to start breathing faster.

"I talked to Pastor Nathan recently, and he said the same thing."

Symone smiled. "That's what you call confirmation. God put the same thing on both our hearts to tell you."

She took my hand. "Pray about this, Jeremiah. And don't just talk to God. Listen to what He has to say."

We walked back to the car holding hands. I'm beyond disappointed, but I still felt comfortable with her. I reflected on our conversation the rest of the ride to her house, and wondered if she was doing the same.

"Last stop, everybody out."

Symone giggled as I opened the car door for her.

"Jeremiah, thanks for taking me out. I really appreciate it. And thanks for not making me walk home after I said what I said to you."

I snickered even as I fumbled for words, not sure what to say next. "You're welcome. Even though this has to be the strangest date I ever went on."

Symone laughed. "What? You mean I'm the first woman you ever went out with who advised you to go talk to another woman? How could that be?"

I tried to laugh, but it came out as a snort.

"Believe me Symone, you're one of a kind."

I looked down at her, and nearly cried at the emotion I saw in her eyes.

"Thank you for caring. Thank you for being obedient to what God told you. I know it wasn't easy for you to tell me all that."

We shared a long hug. "It wasn't. It isn't." Her voice dropped to a whisper. "But I know what's right."

She stood on tiptoe and kissed me on the cheek. "Be blessed, Jeremiah. I'm not going to stop being your friend, but I need you to give me a few days. I need time to sort out my own feelings in all this."

I nodded, unable to speak for the moment. I watched as Symone waved goodbye and waited until she was safely inside before I got back in my car.

This was not exactly how I envisioned this date ending.

I got through the rest of the weekend intact, but Monday was a bear.

I'm not one who hates Mondays, but this one didn't feel all that great. Guess that's what happens when a woman breaks it off with you. That thought haunted me even after I got home.

Thing is, even though Symone struck a nerve when she told me I had unfinished business with Jenisse, I couldn't be mad at her. I wanted to disagree, but I couldn't.

No matter how I felt, I knew that Symone and Pastor were right. But how am I supposed to move on when Jenisse made it clear that she loved me 'like a brother', and Symone won't see me at all?

I thought dating her was what I needed to forget about Jenisse as anything but my sister, but I don't have that option anymore.

Guess I needed to meet someone else. I better not give off that vibe around those Singles Ministry women though. I'm convinced that they could smell blood in the water. If I gave off a vibe that I'm available, one of them might swoop me up in her talons and carry me off to her nest.

The doorbell interrupted me chuckling at that imagery. I opened the door to Erik standing on my doorstep grinning.

"Sorry I couldn't answer your call last night. I was out with Talia, and I had my phone off. Last thing I needed was to answer it instead of paying her all my attention."

"Must be going well, then."

Erik grinned. "Sure is. Valentine's Day is coming fast, and I've got a nice night planned for her."

He outlined plans that included dinner and an elaborate bouquet of roses from a florist who goes to our church.

"How about you? You and Symone gonna paint the town red?"

"Nope."

I described last night, from the great time we had at the movies to the deep conversation over shakes at Jake's.

"So she straight out told you she won't keep going out with you because she can tell you're not over Jenisse? What did you say?"

"What could I say? She's right. And the bad part about that is, we already had our big talk. Nothing I say now will ever convince Jenisse to give us a chance. If we can't resolve what's been between us all this time, Symone will never give me a chance either. It's like I'm running through snowdrifts and trying to get somewhere."

Erik looked me in the eye. "Which one do you want? I mean, if both of them were equally willing to date you, which one would you choose?"

I started to open my mouth, to say Symone of course, but I couldn't. Those words would not come out of my mouth because I didn't believe they were true.

"What the heck is wrong with me? I should be saying Symone, hands down. They're both saved, but Symone is gorgeous, she's sweet, she's not complicated, she's unselfish, she wants children someday and has no problems with abstinence until marriage. If I had my choice, I should be knocking Jenisse over trying to get to Symone. But..."

Erik held his stare. "But?"

"But I can't get Jenisse out of my system. She's high maintenance, she's selfish at times, but at others she's ready to give the blouse off her back. She has a temper, but she knows how to keep it from controlling her. Jenisse is just—more alive."

Erik nodded. "Sounds like you've got some praying to do."

"Praying about this is tops on my list. I definitely need more time if I'm going to get over Jenisse, that's for sure."

I forced a smile so plastic a Ken doll would call it phony. "I really am glad to hear it's going well with you and Talia though. One of us needs to get his happily ever after on. Might as well be you."

"Don't give up Jay. Yours might still come through."

I shook my head. "It took Jenisse and me years to get there, but we finally talked about everything. And even after we talked, she still can't get past all the barriers she put up in her heart. She'll only allow herself to see me as good 'ol Jay. I've had enough. As much as it hurts, I had to let go of Jenisse and move on. I gave it a shot with Symone, but apparently that wasn't meant to be either."

Erik sighed. "I said all along you got issues, and this proves it. When a woman who admitted she wouldn't mind dating you herself tells you that you need to resolve some things, you might want to take that advice. Prayerfully it's only a matter of time before Jenisse catches that same clue. Any way you look at it though, you need to resolve your issues. If you don't, it won't work with Jenisse, Symone or anyone else."

Before Erik left to put the finishing touches on his Valentine's Day plans, he prayed for me, and asked God for both of our happy endings to come through. He opened the door to leave and almost walked right into Joel.

16

I pulled up my guard up as I allowed him in. I had to be careful; he's had me on his Dirt List ever since I repossessed his car and attached his wages.

"Hey, Jay."

I invited him in, still wary of what he might be up to. Not to my surprise Erik retraced his steps and walked in behind Joel.

They chatted for a moment while I got back comfortable in my favorite chair. Joel handed me an envelope.

"You got your first two payments straight from my check, and here's the third. Think you could un-attach my wages now?"

I counted the cash.

"I said once you made those three back payments, we could talk. This is a good start. We've done this before though. You've made one payment and then conveniently forgotten to make any more."

Joel nodded. I put the cash in my wallet, pleased that he made the effort to get the third payment to me a full two weeks before his next paycheck.

"Believe it or not Joel, we're all pulling for you."

Joel rolled his eyes. "Pulling for me. Uh huh. You guys just get off on acting like you're my dad or something."

"Believe it or not, I have better things to do with my life than crack down on you. None of this would've happened if you'd just kept your word and paid me back instead of blowing me off and thinking I wouldn't notice."

Joel glared fire at me. "Easy for you to talk about money; you got plenty of it. Some of us have to work for a living."

"You trifling, selfish son of a..."

I was out of my chair and in Joel's face before I knew it. I snatched him up and slammed him against the wall before my mind registered the action. Erik moved to pull me off of Joel. My side-eye must have been lethal; he stopped in his tracks.

"For some reason, you think the world owes you a living. Let me tell you something, boy. It doesn't!"

Joel tried to break my grip to no avail. "Come on, man. Let go!"

"You're jealous that I got some money and that I only work because I want to. Trust me Joel, I'd rather not have money than get it how I got it."

Joel started to stammer out something, but I cut him off. "Shut up!"

Joel and Erik both turned pale.

I loosened my grip on Joel just a bit and turned to Erik. "After I lost my last family member, the mother you won't talk to now literally saved my life when I stopped being numb and cared enough to think about suicide."

I let Joel go and turned sideways. It's hard to look tough when you're trying not to cry.

I looked at Erik. "Life's too short for this crap, dude. You don't know what tomorrow's gonna bring, and trust me, you don't want to live with any regrets. Quit acting like a butt and go talk to your parents. I've got enough issues without having to be your messenger boy."

I turned back to Joel. "Believe it or not, I'm jealous of you in one respect. You have a wife and kids, but you're taking them for granted. Keep going how you're going, and you might lose them."

Both of them looked as close to tears as I was. When I stopped talking, they left without saying anything else.

That was good. I needed a few minutes to get it together before my company arrived.

"Thanks for letting us come over, Jeremiah. I didn't expect all the church meeting rooms to be taken tonight."

"No problem, Symone. We needed to meet now as opposed to next week if we're going to get this financial seminar planned. Besides, I just had family over and I was glad to have a reason to get rid of them."

Symone and our other committee members laughed out loud. "That bad, huh?"

"When it comes to my brothers, I'm glad twice; when they show up and when they leave."

The meeting went by faster than I thought. After we adjourned, we finished straightening up, and both John and Tracey left, one after the other. Symone declared her intention to be next.

"Not that I don't trust you Jay, but I don't want the rumor mill to get wind of me being here with you alone for any length of time."

"I totally get that."

She asked for the bathroom. After I pointed her in the right direction, I looked around to see if there was any more straightening up I needed to do. These folks wore me out tonight; going to sleep sounded like a good idea after Symone left.

The doorbell rang on cue. Great. If it's one of the family, that would kill early bedtime.

When I opened the door, Jenisse breezed in. Yup, no early sleep for me. That 'we need to talk' look on her face never led to a short conversation.

"Jay, you got a minute. I need some advice."

I didn't let her see me roll my eyes. I'd really rather go to bed, but issues or not, Jenisse was my sister.

"Okay, what's going on now?"

"It's Clarence. I broke up with him."

She launched into the details, but stopped as she fixed a stare on one of my chairs.

"Whose jacket is that?"

Symone chose that moment to emerge from the hallway that led to my downstairs bathroom. "Hi Jenisse."

"And you're here, alone with Jay, why?"

I saw something in her eyes I didn't like. I'm guessing Jenisse connected some dots that didn't exist. Symone must have seen it too. Her brow furrowed, and she aimed a questioning look at Jenisse and then at me.

"Is somebody gonna answer my question?"

Crap. I knew Jenisse was a bit put off by me taking Symone to the dance, but I didn't realize it ran this deep.

Jenisse focused a maniacal glare on Symone. "Okay, I see what's going on here. You made it your business to become friends with me so you could get to him."

She pointed at me. I couldn't summon up a mumbling word. Jenisse then surprised both of us and punctuated her accusation with an epithet so foul that if someone had directed it toward her, it would have provoked a major fistfight.

To her credit, Symone held her temper at being called out of her name and species. I started to say something, but Symone put up a hand and gave me a look that said 'I got this.'

"Jenisse, if I were one of those names you called me, I'd slap both that word and the taste out of your mouth. Or, we can keep our earrings on and discuss this like two grown women. Your choice."

I tensed up, just in case Jenisse made the wrong choice and I had to break up a fight. The steel in Symone's voice and the fire in her eyes negated their four-inch height difference. Jenisse took a deep breath and backed down.

"Thank you. We're much too old to fight over anything. Besides, I'd probably pull a muscle beating you down."

Jenisse looked like she'd just seen Bigfoot riding a unicorn. Symone laughed in response to her expression.

"Don't look so shocked. This isn't what you thought it was. I think Jeremiah's a nice guy, but that's it. Given your extreme reaction, you two need to talk."

Symone retrieved her jacket and purse and let herself out.

"Jay, I'm sorry for...I mean, I shouldn't have...oh God, I can't do this right now!"

Jenisse turned tail and ran from my house. I couldn't move to stop her if I wanted to. I heard her pull away and drive off, but I was rooted to the spot.

Guess I haven't moved on after all.

17

"If *we confess our sins, He is faithful and just to forgive us our sins and to cleanse us from all unrighteousness."*

I reread John 1:9 for about the twentieth time since Pastor Nathan gave it to me to study. I still had time before three of my nieces and nephews got here and I intended to use it wisely. I was still trying to sort through what happened with Jenisse and Symone a few days ago.

Until the Symone/Jenisse face off I thought I'd done a pretty good job of convincing myself I was romantically over Jenisse. But now I'm not so sure if that's true.

"If we confess our sins..."

Okay, I realize how important it was not to try and cover up what we do wrong.

"...to cleanse us from all unrighteousness."

Clarity hit me like a speeding truck. "Oh. My. God."

I couldn't help but drop to my knees.

Lord, forgive me. I didn't want to admit this even to myself, but I never brought this to You because I wanted to keep it and treasure it in my heart.

With that, I reviewed what happened all those years ago for the millionth time, but this time was different. Instead of savoring it like a favorite DVD, I saw it for what it was and was: an offense to God.

Forgive me for my part in it, God. I never should've let Jenisse entice me into her bed. I was the one who had a relationship with You at that time- I should have set her a better example. Forgive me for mistreating your daughter Jenisse.

I was still on my knees when the doorbell rang and the sound of children echoed from the other side of the door. My dates are here.

I opened the door and was rushed by a trio of little ones. Since I had no date for Valentine's, I settled for these ones I knew loved me.

We settled in the rec room and watched Frozen for the 975th time. Amazing how it had the ability to knock these kids out. I don't know why; I just accepted the blessing.

I left the trio on the couch where they passed out and covered them with the Hello Kitty and Ninja Turtle blankets I kept on hand for them.

This wasn't how I saw Valentine's Day happening this year, but then again who could have seen Symone's reaction coming? Oh well, it is what it is.

I wish I could have seen Deborah's face when I told her I couldn't take her kids because Ruth asked me first. I knew I wouldn't get a call from Joel; I heard that he got Jenisse to take the Terrorist Twins.

Crazy as things have been, Jenisse and I e needed to clear the air between us.

The first Sunday dinner at Mama CC's after she tripped out on me and Symone was kinda tense. After that, I stopped coming. I figured they could do without the tension and that Jenisse would enjoy herself again if I wasn't there.

Durn if Ruth didn't tell me Jenisse stopped coming too. It hadn't happened yet, but it won't be long before Mama CC and Mr. Thurman would be on me to make this right.

The problem is that time apart made things more complicated with me and Jenisse. That scene the other day pulled the scab off an old wound we didn't even realize was so deep.

My cell phone rang. I answered it before it could wake up the kids. "Hello?"

The weary, haunted voice on the other end of the phone sounded like the harbinger of impending doom. "Jeremiah?"

Uh oh. She only sounds like that when there's a problem.

"Mama CC? What's wrong?"

I heard the pain of an entire lifetime condensed into one breathy sentence.

"We're at Christiana Hospital. Erik's been hurt."

I bundled up three kids in record time to get to the hospital. They were unusually quiet; after their initial questions about why I woke them up, they fell silent and stayed that way for the entire ride.

I made it into the waiting room half-carrying and half dragging three kids. "What happened? Where is he?"

Mama CC looked thirty years older. Fear and doubt replaced the joy that usually sparkled in her eyes. Mr. Thurman didn't look much better; he was clearly trying to be strong for Mama CC, but it was equally obvious he waged an all-out war against the urge to cry.

"Sit down, Jeremiah. You're the last one to get here. We only wanted to have to say this once."

Every one of us currently living in Delaware beat me here. Jenisse took my three charges and added them to the pile of children sleeping on the nearby couches. They went to sleep almost immediately.

Mr. Thurman put his arm around Mama CC's shoulders and took the job of giving the bad news.

"The police told us an eighteen-wheeler lost control on I-95 and crushed Erik's car against the restraining wall. They haven't given us any specifics yet, but Erik was badly injured. He's in surgery right now, and his condition is critical."

Gasps and small sobs punctuated Mr. Thurman's statement. I'm glad the kids were all out cold and didn't hear that.

"We don't know all the details, but...."

Mr. Thurman's voice choked off, and Mama CC filled in the gap. "The police think the truck driver either fell asleep at the wheel or was intoxicated."

As we assimilated this new information, a thought occurred to me. "Talia."

CC jerked her head up, and Jenisse looked confused. "What?"

"He was on his way to pick up his girlfriend for a date. She needs to know what happened, and I don't have her phone number."

Mama CC reached into her purse. "I have some of Erik's things. His phone was still in one piece. Maybe her number's in there."

I took the phone. "Let me."

Her number was there and I was able to reach her. Mama CC asked me to call Pastor Nathan as well and get the prayer chain going. She and Mr. Thurman called the out of state siblings to get them praying too. Barbara took the opportunity to bid us goodbye. She and Joel carried their girls to the car so she could take them home and put them to bed while Joel stayed with us. Deborah's husband took their children soon after, and volunteered to keep Ruth's as well.

As Mr. Thurman disconnected from the last out-of-state call, Talia burst into the waiting room, eyes red from crying. I nominated myself as welcoming committee; pulled her aside to fill her in and then brought her to the group for full introductions. As I got started with the intros, the door opened again. Symone entered the room behind Joel's return.

"I came as soon as I heard. How is he?"

I needed the hug I gave her as much as she did. "He's in surgery. We're waiting for an update."

Symone slumped down on the couch, unable to hold back tears. Jenisse sat beside her, and embraced her.

"How did you know?"

Symone managed a weak smile. "My brother's a police officer. He was close by when the emergency call went out, and he was at the scene. When he recognized Erik, he called me first chance he got. I couldn't just stay home; I wanted to be here."

Without another word, we stood and formed a prayer circle just as Pastor Nathan entered the room.

"Looks like I arrived just in time."

He led us in prayer. Mama CC, Mr. Thurman and I each took turns praying, and we felt the presence of God moving among us. After prayer, all we could do was wait. It was hours before someone came to give us any information. the Amen, we all felt better in spite of the circumstances. It took us a minute to notice the doctor standing at the back of the room, respectfully awaiting our attention.

"Mr. and Mrs. Dawson?"

We parted like the Red Sea so our folks could get a clear view of the doctor.

"I'm Dr. Edney, Dr. Thorpe's intern. He sent me out to update Mr. and Mrs. Dawson on the condition of their son."

Mr. Thurman stepped forward. "I'm Thurman Dawson. This is my wife CC. How's my boy?"

The doctor ran his hands through thinning blond hair. "Mr. and Mrs. Dawson, Erik is holding on. We successfully repaired his punctured lung. He has a compound fracture of the left leg, which will require surgery. His left shoulder was separated; that was pretty easy to put back in place. He has multiple broken ribs. We've stabilized them. What we won't know for sure is the extent of his neck and spine injuries."

Jenisse and Symone gasped simultaneously.

Mama CC wept softly at this news.

Dr. Edney spoke with a controlled calm. "That's what I have for you medically. Spiritually speaking, Erik is in the hands of a far better Doctor than we are. And, he has you all praying for him."

Mr. Thurman thanked the doctor and slumped into a seat.

Mama CC moved to hug Pastor Nathan. "Thank you for coming, Pastor."

"I wouldn't be anywhere else. I'll stay or leave as you need me to, but I felt that I needed to come and pray with you in person right now."

I stayed close to Mama CC and Mr. Thurman. They're always strong for all of us, but now they needed us to be strong for them. I knew what they would have done for someone else if it were their child lying near death, and I took on that role for them. I worked the room on their behalf; brought Ruth some tissues, gave Deborah a hug, spoke some encouragement to Joel. And then I got to Jenisse.

"You okay?"

"No. This waiting is tough to deal with. And, I keep wondering how he'll look."

Okay, this is no time for me to let my issues get in the way. She needs me. "Do you, I mean, well, I'll go in with you. If you want me to. When it's time."

Jenisse blinked in surprise. "Um, yeah. Thanks."

I'll say this for my family; they know how to circle the wagons and they aren't petty. Despite the fact that nobody but me knew Talia existed before Erik's accident.

"I sh-should've called him sooner."

Symone rubbed Talia's back. "There's nothing you could have done to change this. Don't blame yourself."

"I put him off for years. We could have been together all this time, and now it might be too late!"

As Talia dissolved into more tears, Jenisse stiffened as if hit with a quarterstaff. She'd edged closer to help, only to take an emotional blow from overhearing that conversation. Looked like Talia's talk about romantic convenience hit Jenisse dead center and stuck like an arrow. I put a comforting hand on Jenisse's shoulder, she leaned into me as she always did. I let her rest her head on my shoulder the way I used to without hesitation. I guided her to a seat and we settled in to wait.

I jerked awake and realized I had no clue where I was. Jenisse's head lifted off my shoulder. We stared at each other until I remembered where we were.

"No Dorothy, you aren't in Kansas anymore."

I remembered where I was, started to I started to laugh at Mama

CC's statement and coughed instead. Fortunately, I'd left a bottle of water where I could reach it; my throat was drier than political humor.

"Guess I couldn't play that off, huh?"

Mama CC laughed and woke up Mr. Thurman. "Not hardly."

All my brain cells kicked in and I remembered that we sent everyone home while Jenisse and I stayed at the hospital with Mama CC and Mr. Thurman.

The sight of Dr. Edney approaching shook the four of us out of the last remnants of sleep. *Dear God, let him have good news!*

Dr. Edney smiled. "We'll do the best we can. We're waiting on results from Erik's MRI so we can assess the extent of his spinal injuries."

With that information, there was nothing to do now but wait.

Mama CC reached for her purse. "Jeremiah, I think this would be a good time for you and Jenisse to take a break from all this."

If I had the same deer-in-the-headlights look on my face as Jenisse had on hers, no wonder the folks laughed.

"Erik'll be fine. She pointed upward. "He's in good hands."

I turned to Jenisse. "Didn't Joel and Barbara bring you here?"

Jenisse's head snapped up, "Yeah."

"I thought so. I'll take you back to their house to get your car before I head home."

18

"**J**ay, we need to talk."

I took a deep breath as we drove to get her car.

"Understatement of the century. We do, but I'm really tired and I don't think now is the time."

Jenisse lowered her head. "You're right. Look, we both need to get a shower and a nap at the least. Call me when you wake up. We'll go back and see Erik when they say it's okay, and as soon as we can get a few spare minutes, we will talk. I promise I won't run or avoid or go seventh grade on you this time."

I woke up suddenly, not quite sure what time it was or what I should be doing instead of sleeping. I reached for my cell phone, but only managed to knock it off my night table and send it skittering out of my reach. I got up, found it and noticed that it was five in the evening. I'd slept about six hours.

Time to eat.

I had just finished a sandwich and a bowl of Honey Nut Cheerios when my cell rang. Jenisse.

"He's awake!"

That's all I needed to hear. I was out the door and headed to the hospital in record time.

Jenisse and I barely cleared the door waiting room door at the same time. Mama CC gave us the good news.

"He came through his surgery just fine. It was a long wait but he's out of recovery and we were able to see him for a brief minute. The doctors say he's still in serious condition, but he's doing better than they thought he would."

She looked at her watch. "Thurman went to get us something to drink. They took him to the ICU. We' can check to see if they'll let you guys see him."

I looked at Jenisse, and she took my hand as we walked towards Intensive Care. To our pleasure we were allowed in.

We went in slow. I braced myself for the worst. We weren't disappointed. My first sight of Erik almost caused me to turn around and leave the room.

His skin was pale, and he was attached to more machines than I knew existed. A respirator assisted his breathing, and his multiple broken bones were immobilized by various means.

Erik's eyes fluttered open as we drew near.

"Man, you done did it now. You stood Talia up on Valentine's Day. Unless you have a real good excuse, she's gonna do you worse than this when she gets the chance."

Jenisse chuckled, and I thought I saw a smile in Erik's eyes.

"We're praying for you, man. And we need you to get better so you can pray for us too."

A single tear rolled down his cheek before his eyes fluttered closed again.

We slipped out of the room to let him rest. We ran into Joel and Barbara's in the waiting area. Rather than crowd the small area, Jenisse and I took advantage of the nice weather and took a walk.

After an awkward silence Jenisse broke the silence. "Jay, I'm sorry. I've been unfair to you for years now, but I couldn't admit that to myself because I wasn't happy with who I was."

She laughed humorlessly and stared straight ahead. I saw unshed tears pooled in the corner of her eyes.

"I'd convinced myself that nobody worth having would want to be with me for more than a night or two, and I set out to prove it. I also had myself convinced it would change someday. In my heart, I knew that a fine man would be out there waiting for me, and that meeting him would make up for all the losers I went through to get to him."

My pulse raced; I almost had to clamp my mouth shut to keep from interrupting.

"I've always thought I could do whatever I wanted if I put my mind to it. When I realized how much of a ho I'd become, I stopped sleeping around. When the doctor told me I had to lose weight to avoid knee surgery, I changed my eating habits and started working out. Being celibate and losing hundred and five pounds didn't happen overnight, but it happened. I said all the right things and gave God lip service credit, but in my heart, I took credit for it. I did it. It was because I was all that, and I treated my feelings for you the same way. Because I did all the right things, I expected the man God set aside for me to look like that image I had in my head."

Images of tall black men ranging in color from high yellow to obsidian and all in between raced through my head. Jenisse's men over the years all had one thing in common; they were six feet tall or over, athletically built and movie star handsome. She had been with men who could have face-doubled for movie star eye candy. And I don't look like that.

"Jay, when you opened up to me, it scared me to death. I always knew you liked me, but I didn't let myself believe you loved me until we finally talked things out. And even then, I was afraid to take it any further than talking. I couldn't let myself admit I had those kind of feelings for you because it was dangerous. I couldn't take the chance that you'd turn out to be counterfeit like the other men I've known."

"What changed your mind?"

"I heard something Talia told Symone. It cut me to my heart when she said she may have waited too long to let Erik know she cares about him."

Jenisse drew a ragged breath. "I don't want it to be too late for us, Jay."

I couldn't stop a tear from rolling down my cheek. "Neither do I."

I started to get up, changed my mind and settled into the chair, only to shift position again a second later.

"Jay, this has been the most insane day and a half I've ever had. I'm still trying to process it all, but if there's anything good that's come out of all this, it's us."

I let that loaded comment hang in the air for a moment.

"I kind of got the memo when I acted a butt fool with you and Symone, but this situation with Erik made it more real. Life is way too short to play games. I've been taking you for granted all these years."

I couldn't speak. I'd been waiting over ten years to hear her say those words. I wanted to shout for joy, but even as I felt my heart lighten, I felt a check in my spirit.

"I've spent years believing every lie the devil ever told me; believing

I really was a fat ho, believing I didn't deserve the love of a good man or to be treated well in a relationship."

Jenisse brushed her lips lightly across mine. My toes curled up.

"I was wrong. God and everyone I knew had been telling me for years how you felt about me, but I couldn't accept it because that would have meant admitting to myself how I feel about you. Jay, I'm tired of settling for less. I want every blessing God has for me- and you're one of them."

"Be still, and know that I am God."

I almost missed the still, silent voice that dropped into my spirit, but as I processed the words, I knew what I had to say and do.

"Jenisse, I know it was hard for you to open up the way you did, and I'm glad you felt able to trust me with, with everything."

I took a deep breath. "This is tough for me to say, so I'll just spit it out. We can't do this. Not right now."

Jenisse looked as though someone asked her to read a legal brief written in Mandarin Chinese.

"Jenisse, you do deserve to be loved. You do deserve to be respected, and you do deserve to be treated like a queen. I've waited years for you to believe it to be so, and I've learned something through the waiting."

I took a deep breath, and sat tall. I felt a supernatural boldness fill me, and encouraged me to keep talking.

"Ten years ago we had a similar conversation and we wound up in bed together. If we were to start something now, I believe it would be just as big of a mistake."

Jenisse managed to find her voice. "Why?"

"You and I have come a long way, but we still have more ground to cover. You do deserve the best, and so do I. The boy who ran behind you all this time is now a man. I deserve a woman who's able to be for me what I've been for you all these years. Are you that woman right now?"

I don't think so."

"Are you capable of becoming that woman?"

"I believe yes. I just don't want to take advantage of you ever again."

I quoted the Bible verse had convicted me. "If we confess our sins, He is faithful and just to forgive us our sins and to cleanse us from all unrighteousness. That's from I John 1:9. Pastor had me meditate on that verse. Doing so led me to this one." I quoted I Corinthians 13:4-8. "Love suffers long and is kind; love does not parade itself, is not puffed up; does not behave rudely, does not seek its own, is not provoked, thinks no evil, does not rejoice in iniquity, but rejoices in the truth; bears all things, believes all things, hopes all things, endures all things. Love never fails."

I took her hands into mine. "Jenisse, I love you, but I know without a doubt that us trying to get together right now would be another mistake. Our hearts have to belong to Christ before they can belong to each other. We're not ready yet."

"Then I heard a loud voice saying in heaven, 'Now salvation and strength and the kingdom of our God, and the power of His Christ have come, for the accuser of our brethren, who accused them before our God day and night, has been cast down. And they overcame him by the blood of the Lamb and by the word of their testimony, and they did not love their lives to the death."

As Jenisse quoted scripture, I looked like I'd seen Superman fly overhead.

"What? You think you're the only one seeking God in all this?"

Our laughter shattered the tension.

"Revelation 12:10-11. Sister Nathan had me memorize it after our first counseling session. I've been meditating on it ever since, and I think I'm just now starting to fully understand why."

"Jenisse, I can't tell you what it is the devil is still accusing you of. All I can do is pray that you'll confront that thing the way you're dealing with our situation. Don't be afraid to let God show you exactly what it is in your life that's blocking you, and when you see it, deal with it. That scripture you just quoted me says it all. You're set free by the blood of Jesus. Now you have to confess to God whatever it is you're still not letting go of. I can't do that for you. This has to be between you and God."

19

I felt better than I had in years. I had fasted the past twelve hours, and when I wasn't at work, I was in the Word. I read I John over and over. That alone kept me from picking up the phone and making the call I knew I had no business making.

I had to let Jenisse get to where she needed to be on her own.

I prayed aloud. "God, thank you for helping me stay the course and not go running right back to her the first time I missed her. Or now. It's been three months, and I need to hold to your path even if it takes ten more.

As I closed my Bible and went back into prayer, I John 1:9 echoed in my spirit. But this time is more like unfinished business. I'd confessed my sin and I know You've forgiven to me. What else can I do?

You never asked hers.

My eyes widened with dawning comprehension. Tears stung my eyes and I went back to praying.

"God, thank You for all You revealed to me."

Jenisse stayed on my mind. I wondered if she was going through something. If so, I felt I was helping her the best way I knew how. When it's time for us to talk again, God would let me know. And when we do talk, I have a lot more to say.

Until that time, I'd continue to pray and seek pastoral counseling. That path changed in a way I hadn't anticipated.

Pastor He moved me from one counseling session per week to two, and it has really helped me.

Today we dealt with my Messiah complex and why I felt like I needed to rescue everybody from whatever situation they swore they needed me to get them out of. When we dug deeper, the truth came out.

I couldn't save my dad from a heart attack or keep my mother from falling into depression after her first stroke. Since then I had unconsciously tried to save everybody else. That was why I let Jenisse run me for so long.

Another good thing for me was the space between us. Not having Jenisse up under me all the time also gave me the chance to consider a career move. I liked my current job, but now I had a really good offer on the table. I've kept it in prayer, talked to Pastor Nathan about it and it felt right. I'm thinking I should take it.

I was about to get in my car when a woman spoke from behind me and scared me half to death.

"Jay?"

My head jerked up.

"Jenisse! Haven't seen you in a while. How've you been?"

She smiled and we shared an awkward hug. The last time we had a meaningful conversation was that amazing talk we had three months ago. I'd missed being around her on a regular basis, but we needed not to be up under each other. I've learned the accuracy of that quote: "Absence makes the heart grow fonder." It had for me.

"Blessed. God's been dealing with me on a lot of things, and it feels good to actually listen to Him for a change."

I laughed. "Who you telling?"

She pointed back to the church. "I'm, well I'm here to see Sister Nathan. More counseling."

I chuckled. "I just came out of a session with Pastor. It's enlightening to say the least."

Jenisse fiddled with her purse strap. "I'm sorry to hear about what happened with Symone."

"Stuff happens."

Hard to be nonchalant when you're thoroughly disgusted with a situation. About ten seconds after Jenisse and I had our latest talk, I started talking to Symone again. Unlike me, she was smart enough to figure out I was still dealing with Jenisse-related issues and still refused to date me. Before I knew it, she met someone else.

"She's really happy with him. They've been together almost two months now, and it looks like the real thing. How can I begrudge her that?"

Jenisse smiled wanly. "You can't. If anyone deserves a good man, Symone does."

She paused, struggling for words. "Jay, I talked to my mother."

"Really? When did this happen?"

"It was maybe two weeks after Erik's accident. We got to a lot of stuff out there that I'd been holding onto for years. I finally told her how mad I was all my life because she always chose men over me, starting with my deadbeat dad."

I snapped my head up. "Whoa."

"That was the root of why I acted the way I did around men. I hated how Mom treated me and how she threw herself at every man she was interested in, yet I did the exact same thing when I got old enough to date. Isn't that a mess? I hated how my mother acted, and I turned into her anyway."

"I'm glad you went and talked to her."

"Blame your pastor." Jenisse smiled. "If he didn't make us say the Ten Commandments every Sunday, I wouldn't have gotten stuck on 'Honor thy father and thy mother.' I couldn't get that verse out of my head, and when Erik almost died without making it right with Mama CC, I knew I had to go talk to my mom. I mean, what if something happened to her? It's bad enough my dad died before we could talk; I didn't want to take the chance on losing Mom too."

Jenisse chuckled. "She might go back to not talking if I keep making her work out with me. Mom made the mistake of telling me her doctor said she needs to lose thirty pounds or she's at risk to develop diabetes. I'm gonna make sure she at least tries."

I had to laugh. "At least she has an expert to work with."

I saw the regret in Jenisse's eyes. I'm pretty sure she could see it in mine.

"Jay, you were right. When we had that talk a few months back, I thought I was finally ready to be the woman in your life, but I still had to deal with some things, starting with my mother. Sister Nathan helped me see that, and not too long after we talked is when I went to see my mom so we could clear the air between us. That was the main thing I hadn't dealt with- being mad at my mother for giving me a lousy dad to work with."

She chuckled, and I joined her.

"After I talked to Mom, I went to Grace Lawn to visit his grave. That conversation was a bit one-sided though."

That cracked me up.

"I did get some things off my chest. I forgave him, Jay. I wish I could explain what a weight it is off my back now that I've done it."

She took a deep breath. "Jay, I took you for granted ever since we met. And if that wasn't bad enough, I seduced you and then refused to talk about it. I put you through more emotional hell than anyone should have to endure. Can you ever forgive me?"

"Yes, I forgive you. And I need you to forgive me too. Jenisse, I'm sorry."

Jenisse gave me a blank look. "*You're* sorry? For *what?*"

I took her hands. "I'm sorry you've had such a bad time with men. I saw for myself how a lot of them, a lot of *us*, treated you, and it was wrong. Whether you offered yourself or not, none of us had the right to treat you like a toy."

Jenisse was speechless.

"They're not here to apologize, but I am. On behalf of every man who ever used you, including me, I apologize. I'm sorry."

Jenisse tried to speak again, but couldn't. I held her and let her cry.

When the deluge ended, she reached for a tissue and blew her nose.

I chuckled. "Way to kill a tender moment."

She punched me lightly on the arm.

"Jay, you don't know what that meant to me. I've had a lot of people do a lot of shady things to me over the years. I never told anybody this, but all I've ever wanted was for somebody to apologize. It didn't matter who; my father, my mother, the girls who always talked about me, the men who knew I was looking for something permanent and used me for sex anyway; I just wanted to hear somebody say "I'm sorry" to me and mean it."

Jenisse looked at me like she was seeing me for the first time.

"Pastor taught me something else too. He showed me that I had to let you go."

Jenisse's hopeful smile dropped into a near pout fell as my words sank in.

"I didn't realize it, but I put all my hopes in you and cut God out of the equation. That was all wrong. You're my girl and all, but you didn't die for my sins!"

I saw hope return to her face, and we laughed together for the first time in months.

"Pastor taught me that this is where a lot of men and women go wrong. We put our relationships with other people on a pedestal and it becomes more important to us than our relationship with God."

Jenisse perked up. "Sister Nathan told me the same thing! And she's right. When I slept around, I was looking for something, but I was looking wrong. I needed Jesus, not new men."

She drew another deep breath. "Once I let go of loose sex, I needed something to lean on. Instead of asking Jesus to guide me, I relied on you to make everything all right."

She swallowed hard, and forced her next words out. "I've always known how you feel about me. I knew I wasn't ready or able to respond like you wanted and I took advantage of you anyway. Ever since I can remember, I leaned on you to get me through the hard times. I knew you'd always be there for me, but for my sake and yours I had to learn how to make it on my own. I couldn't do that while holding onto you so tight you couldn't breathe."

I tried to look stern. "If you apologize again, I'm gonna hurt you."

More laughter.

"Let me make this plain, Jenisse. I love you. I've spent the past three months learning how to do that the right way, and I've still got more learning to do. I hope we can do that learning together going forward."

"I'd like that. The thought of 'us' doesn't seem so scary anymore."

I nodded. "Pastor and his wife do couples counseling. I think we should sign up."

"Definitely. It's taken us a long time to get to this point. I don't want to mess it up."

I took a deep breath. "It's going to get complicated though. I got a job offer."

She smiled. "Let me guess. Mama CC again?"

I nodded. "Yup. She keeps offering me the chance to serve as Chief Financial Officer for one of her branches, and until now, I've kept turning them down. This time I'm gonna take it."

Jenisse's eyes lit up. "That's great! I've always thought you'd make a good CFO. Now you get to prove it."

"That I do. I just wasn't ready to take the challenge until now."

I took a deep breath. This is harder than I thought it would be. "And I also wasn't ready to move out of state."

Jenisse's eyes widened. "You're taking one of the new ones?"

"Mama told me which branches had a need and described each

position in detail. She's given me all the time I need to pray and decide which one's the best for me right now. "

I looked Jenisse in the eye. "I don't want to get away from you, but I don't want to relapse into being everything to everybody, and I'm definitely ready to do something just for me."

Jenisse nodded.

"I'm going to miss living in the same state with you, but I feel like God is calling me to this particular branch. I'm going to Atlanta."

Jenisse's mouth formed into a perfect O.

"Mama CC and whoever she picks to be Chief Operating Officer will have that branch up and running in the next six months. That'll give me time to give notice at my job here, pack up my whole life and move to Atlanta by the end of the summer."

"Jay, this is…wow. I hardly know what to say."

"I know the timing isn't what we'd want. I mean, we're trying to start something and I drop this on you. But, if you and I are meant to be, it will happen. We might not know how, but God does."

Jenisse smiled her "I know something you don't!" smile. "He does. And I do too. Jay, I'm stepping up to the plate too. Mama CC made me an offer I couldn't refuse. I'm going to be a COO!"

I gave her a high five. "Look at you! Here I thought she was still just offering you Office Manager and she done raised the stakes. Let me guess- you're taking Philadelphia. Mama told me their COO gave notice. Are you taking that spot?"

Again with that smile. "Nope! Her Chicago COO was born here and wants to move back closer to home. She's going to take over in Philly. Mama's promoting Chicago's next in line to take over there. Thing is, she was under consideration for a COO spot elsewhere. Down South to be exact."

I felt my eyes widen. "You don't say."

"Mmm hmm. Since Chicago's staying put, there's now an opening for a COO in Atlanta."

She extended her hand for a formal handshake. "I'm your new boss. Welcome to the team."

I shook her hand formally and then pulled her into a huge hug. The hug somehow became a kiss, which I enjoyed for a few seconds before ending.

"Do you plan to welcome all your executive staff like that?"

She laughed. "Only the ones I have an illicit past with. And since the other officers are women, you're it."

20

Six Months Later

"Hey, wake up! We're almost there."

Jenisse blinked in surprise.

I laughed at her. "Only you could fall asleep in the car on a fifteen-minute ride. Been hitting the clubs again?"

Jenisse rolled her eyes. "Whatever."

Man, I'd missed this. We always had an easy rapport well, at least while we were avoiding our deep issues. That first month after we got back together was awkward, but Pastor Nathan was right. Praying together daily helped us get the old friendly feelings back and then to move further. Weekly couples counseling hadn't hurt anything either.

We need every bit of counseling we could get. Not only are we working on our relationship, but at the same time, we're getting ready to move to Atlanta and take our new jobs.

"This is nice."

"Definitely is. I wasn't comfortable not being comfortable with you."

That gave her a fit of the giggles for some reason.

I managed to find a parking space near Mama CC's house. As soon as I helped Jenisse out of the car, I smiled at her.

"Okay, checklist time."

Jenisse fell into our routine of the past month and pretended to pull out a notepad.

"Quit our jobs here?"

"Check."

"Travel arrangements to Atlanta in a month to start setting up the branch?"

"Check."

"Confirm the temporary housing that Mama set up?"

"Check."

"Marry me before we go?"

Jenisse's head snapped up from her imaginary writing. "What?"

"We survived couples counseling with Pastor and his wife and they agreed we're ready for marriage. Why not get married before we go? We can have Pastor perform a small, quiet ceremony and have a bigger one later, after we get Atlanta up and running."

"And cheat our family out of a huge wedding?"

"You're actually making my point for me."

We laughed. "Seriously though Jenisse, think about it. We're about to be busier than a one legged man in a butt kicking contest. If we don't get married now, we're gonna have to wait at least a year to do the major production we were talking about. And frankly I don't want to wait that long to marry you."

Jenisse looked me in the eye with such tenderness I thought I'd cry. "Jay, it took me awhile to figure this out. Over the years, I let a lot of men touch my body. You're the only one who ever touched my heart."

"Jenisse, I fell in love with you the day we met. You were my first, and you are my only. Will you marry me?"

After trying unsuccessfully to say something twice, she gave up on speaking, pulled me up and kissed the breath out of me.

"I'll take that as a yes."

"Sir Grins-A-Lot's here!"

I rolled my eyes at Erik as we cleared the front door. "That was funny the first three hundred times you said it. Now however…"

Erik grinned and wheeled himself back towards the kitchen, balancing a casserole dish in his lap. "If you're sick of hearing it, then hide them teefus when you come around me. Every time I see you, you're grinning like you just won the Powerball and a date with Halle Berry."

Jenisse smacked Erik on the back of his head. "Halle would have to get in line."

We laughed and helped Mama CC get the food transferred from the kitchen to the dining room table. When she shooed us out of the kitchen to finish the rest herself, I wheeled Erik to one side for a quick chat.

"Is Talia coming?"

Erik shook his head wistfully. "We broke up."

I winced. "Sorry to hear that. I take it she's not handling your recovery as well as you are."

"No."

That one word contained ten years of pain. *God, is it too much to ask that Erik and I can have a happily ever after at the same time?*

"I'll keep praying for you, E. I know God has something great in store for you."

Erik nodded wistfully. "Keep saying it, Jay. These days I need to be reminded of that more and more often."

The rest of the family trickled in a few at a time, with Joel and his family as the last to arrive. They took their places around the table with practiced ease.

CC stood and smiled radiantly. "I'm glad everybody could make it."

She looked at me holding Jenisse's hand under the table and smiled. I bet she saw us out the window before we came in.

"Before we get to why *I* wanted us to celebrate, I think Jeremiah has something to say."

Yeah, she saw us. I stood, and pulled Jenisse up with me. "We're getting married!"

The room exploded with joy. As Jenisse happily displayed the ring, I looked at Erik.

"I was gonna ask you to stand up for me, but..."

Erik shifted in his wheelchair and side-eyed me. "All right now, don't make me get up."

We all laughed.

"As a matter of fact..."

To everyone's surprise, Erik locked the wheels of his chair, braced himself and rose unsteadily to his feet. Everybody gasped and then applauded again.

Mama CC beamed. "This is why I wanted us to celebrate today."

"Remember when the doctors said I'd be paralyzed from the neck down?" Erik smiled. "Clearly 'they' don't know my God. I'm still in this chair, but they took my physical therapy up a notch last week. By the end of the year, I expect to walk again!"

Shouts of praise filled the room as Erik sat back down again, clearly exhausted by the exertion.

"I don't know which was the bigger miracle: my health, me getting over acting a donkey and apologizing to Mom or these two knuckleheads finally figuring out they love each other!"

As our siblings mobbed the three of us, Mama CC and Mr. Thurman sat back and watched. The smiles on their faces spoke volumes.

Epilogue

Six Months Later

"Icaught the bouquet!"

I smiled to see Erik's new girlfriend holding the bouquet with a triumphant grin on her face. She should smile, she's shorter than Erik and somehow managed not to get mauled by the overly eager woman to her left.

I nudged Jenisse and laughed. "Look familiar? Nah, she didn't elbow anybody out of the way to get it."

"Shut up."

I herded Erik toward the dance floor for the garter toss and almost laughed my butt off when, like his girlfriend, he almost got mauled in the process of catching the garter. Didn't think dudes fought over it like that.

I had to pull him away from a tall brother with sharp elbows before he got beaten back into the hospital.

"Come on, dude, you need to go put this on your date. No need to knuckle up over something you didn't want in the first place. I saw you about to step out the way."

"Step out the way is one thing. Get knocked out the way is another."

Erik grumbled some more, but let guide him to where his girlfriend sat, waiting for him to get there with the garter. I left him to his task, found Jenisse and made a circuit of the room. We greeted each table in turn. So far so good- nobody seemed ready to murder us for eloping and not giving them the major production until now.

It's been a good year. We got settled in Atlanta in record time and did our best to get Mama CC's newest branch of Lydia Enterprises up and running. We came back to Delaware to have the long-delayed wedding reception for our family and friends. It happened to fall six months to the day when we announced our engagement at that family dinner.

The family had to adjust to our move out of state. Joel and Barbara took it the hardest- they lost the only two living human beings willing to watch their girls any time they asked. But, they got something else out of the deal. Joel surprised me by making the rest of his payments on time and by throwing in a little extra when he could. He cleared his debt to me last week, and I gave him back his car when we arrived yesterday.

When I got to the table where Erik and his date sat, pangs of jealousy hit. He, his two new best friends and their dates laughed like they'd known each other all their lives. Erik met Garvey and Sam not long after I moved. I feel so replaced.

When we completed our circuit, I caught Erik's eye and signaled him to return to the head table.

I tapped my knife against my glass to shut these loud folks up. "May I have your attention please?"

"I want to thank you all for coming. Jenisse and I appreciate your being here on our special day. The vow renewal ceremony was beautiful, nobody acted ghetto."

Laughter rippled across the room.

"But, today is also special because of the presence of my friends and family."

I looked around the room. "My family. We may not be blood kin, but you wouldn't know it by how much they've loved and supported me over the years."

I introduced Mama CC and Mr. Thurman, and then the rest of the family.

"They came from all over the country to be here today, and I want y'all to see who they are. Stand up, wherever you are."

All of them obliged, amid applause from the other guests.

"And, there's one more. Without his willingness to share his mom and dad with a bunch of total strangers, there wouldn't be an extended family. Ladies and gentlemen, may I present Ant-Man- oops, I mean my brother and best man Erik Dawson!"

Erik gave me the side-eye. "All right now, don't make me get up. You know I can do it now."

Everybody roared with laughter. Erik stood and took the microphone.

"Since Jeremiah called me out, I suppose I should do my job as best man. I'd like to propose this toast to Jeremiah and Jenisse. It took them long enough to get together- now that they are, may God always bless their love as they start their lives together- finally!"

Everyone laughed again, clinked glasses of sparkling cider and drank the toast. Someone tapped a knife against their glass, the signal for us to share a kiss. Like we needed a reason. And the second we came up for air, some clown tapped again.

"They keep this up, we might not be here for the whole reception."

I had to laugh. "A bit eager, are we?"

Jenisse narrowed her eyes at me. "Actually I am, but not for the reason you think."

Just then the MC informed everyone that it was time for the ceremonial first dance. Jenisse sat up straighter in her chair, unable to keep a smile from her face.

"Ahh, now I get it. You're dying for me to know the mystery tune you chose as "our song."

We strutted to the dance floor amid gales of applause. My eyes widened when I recognized the tune: Vanessa Williams' Save The Best For Last.

"Do you like it?"

Goober Grin resurfaced. "I love it! What made you choose it?"

"Because it's what I did with you."

Just then, the MC ordered the wedding party to the dance floor, I caught Erik's eye as he danced with his girlfriend and winked. He side-eyed me, but didn't take his attention off of his dance partner. Maybe. Just maybe.

Jenisse regained my attention and looked me in the eye.

"Over the years, I went through a whole lot of men. I was looking for Mr. Right, but I didn't know I already had him."

She put a hand on my cheek. Funny, I didn't know I knew how to blush.

"I did just what Vanessa Williams is singing about- I saved the best for last."

That earned her another breathtaking kiss. I waited twenty years for this, and it's well worth it.

Mr. Thurman and Mama CC danced by and rewarded us with huge smiles.

Jenisse looked their way. "I want us to be like them when we grow up."

I laughed. "I think we're off to a good start."

I stopped talking and lost myself in the warmth of Jenisse's body and the flow of the music.

- END –

Discussion Questions

1) Why was Jeremiah so willing to go far beyond the call of duty to help his siblings?

2) Was Jeremiah more of a help to his play siblings or a hindrance?

3) How much impact did Joel have on Jeremiah's decision to change?

4) If Jeremiah hadn't challenged the status quo, how long do you think Jenisse would have let things stay as they were?

5) Jeremiah was the first to be mentored by the Dawsons. Did he in any way figure into Erik's feeling that his parents didn't have enough time for him?

6) Was Symone right not to date Jeremiah when he asked her?

7) How important was it for Jeremiah and Jenisse to let go of past hurts?

8) Why do you think Jeremiah and Jenisse were able to stay in a holding pattern in their relationship for as long as they did?

9) Did Jeremiah go too far in how he dealt with Joel or not far enough?

10) Should the Dawsons have done more to push Jeremiah and Jenisse out of their comfort zones?

FEMALE PROBLEMS

Want to see more of Erik? His story continues in Female Problems, due for a September 2016 release through Brown Girls Books.

Thirty-year-old Erik Dawson survived a car crash at the cost of his mobility, his car, his job and his girlfriend. Erik's faith is tested as his body heals and he seeks to rejoin the living.

Sam Sanders is tall, handsome and gainfully employed. He's active in his church, with his fraternity and in his community, yet he can't keep a woman to save his life. At twenty-eight, even he is starting to wonder why he isn't married yet.

Garvey Flowers pursues a career in comedy and a relationship with a woman like none he's ever known, both of which simultaneously motivate and frustrate him.

After a chance encounter brings them together, these three brothers in Christ form an unbreakable bond. They keep each other honest as they explore issues of faith and career goals, and wonder if they will ever truly understand the women in their lives.

This is Book One in the Three Strands series